Maltaverne

FRANÇOIS MAURIAC

Maltaverne

(Un adolescent d'autrefois)

TRANSLATED BY

JEAN STEWART

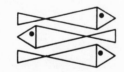

Farrar, Straus and Giroux

New York

Published in French under the title *Un adolescent d'autrefois*,
© Flammarion, 1969
This translation *Maltaverne* © 1970 Eyre & Spottiswoode
Library of Congress catalog card number: 70-113774
Second printing, 1970
Printed in the United States of America

'I write otherwise than I speak,
I speak otherwise than I think,
I think otherwise than I ought to think,
and so on into the deepest heart of darkness'

KAFKA

Maltaverne

I

I am unlike other boys. If I were like other boys, at seventeen I should go shooting with Laurent, my elder brother, and Duberc, our bailiff, and Simon Duberc his younger son, who is an abbé and who at this time of day ought to be at vespers, and Prudent Duberc, his brother, who prompts Simon to make his bow to the curé. I should know how to use a twenty-four-calibre gun instead of beating the bushes and acting like a dog – instead of pretending to be a dog.

Yes, I'm pretending to be a dog, but at the same time I'm wondering what's going on in Simon's head. He has tucked up his soutane on account of the rushes and branches; why are his thick calves in their black woollen stockings so ridiculous? He loves hunting as the gun-dogs Diane and Stop love it; it's in his blood, he can't help it, but he knows that at this time of day Monsieur le Doyen, who is serving Mass, is staring at the empty stall where Simon ought to be but is not. After vespers, M. le Doyen will come to our house to talk to Mother about it. I hope I shall be home by then, although they mistrust me and stop talking as soon as I come near. I talk a lot of nonsense, according to Mother, and M. le Doyen thinks I'm perverse because I ask myself questions that he has never asked himself, that nobody, least of all myself, has ever asked him; but he knows that I think him stupid.

'You think everybody stupid!' Mother scolds me. At home, it's quite true, no one seems intelligent except myself, but I know that I don't know anything because I have been taught nothing. My teachers had nothing to teach me beyond the rudiments of knowledge. My schoolfellows are better than I am at everything that matters to them. They despise me, and they've every reason to despise me; I play no games, I'm as weak as a chicken. I blush when they talk about girls and if they pass round photos I turn my head away. And yet some of them are friendly to me, even more than friendly.

They know what they're going to do, they have jobs waiting for them. But as for me, I don't know what I am. I'm well aware that the things M. le Doyen preaches and my mother believes bear no relation to reality. I know they have no sense of justice. I loathe the religion they practise. All the same I cannot do without God. That's what makes me different, deep down, from all the rest, and not the fact that I play at being a dog and beat the bushes instead of shooting with Laurent and with Prudent and Simon Duberc, and that I'm not even capable of using a twenty-four-calibre gun. Everything that M. le Doyen says seems to me idiotic, and so does the way he says it; and yet I believe it's true, I might almost dare to assert I know it's true, as if a blind man who was at the same time a professional guide might lead me to the real truth, by absurd paths, mumbling Latin and making others mumble it after him, though there are fewer and fewer of them and, in the end, a flock that's barely capable of grazing where he leads it. But then, they walk in the light without seeing it, while I see it, or rather it's within me already. Let them say whatever they like: they are the dunces, the idiots that infuriate my friend Donzac, who is a modernist. All the same, what they believe is true. There you have the whole history of the Church, as I see it.

They got the hare on the edge of Jouanhaut's field. The trek back was exhausting: seven kilometres along that gloomy road that I'm so fond of, between two walls of pine trees: 'as far as you can see, it all belongs to Madame!' Duberc invariably proclaims all along the road, with that extraordinary muzhik's pride of his . . . It's horrible to be writing this. I knew beforehand that on the way back I should have Simon, the abbé, walking beside me in silence. It was Laurent, now, who suddenly turned childish; he began kicking a pine-cone in front of him; if he got it all the way home he'd have won.

Simon and I never talk about anything. He must have heard the curé complain of my perversity, and Simon admires me for being able, at seventeen, to disturb that narrow-minded man under whose thumb he will be so long as he is a seminarist on holiday.

Here I am going to admit, before God, that I'm an impostor: if the Doyen is afraid of me, if Simon admires me, maybe, it's on account of some vague notions I've picked up from my friend André Donzac; he's always dinning into my ears what he's read in the *Annales de philosophie chrétienne*. He's enthusiastic about a certain Père Laberthonnière, an Oratorian who edits this review, and whose very name makes our Doyen see red: 'he's a modernist, he smells of the stake.' I despise the curé for using that cruel, stupid image: the stake! They're ready to burn anyone who believes with his eyes open.

I am an impostor, none the less, since I bombard them with André's inflammatory comments as though they were my own, and pretend to know more than they do, although I'm as abysmally ignorant as they are . . . No, I'm unfair to myself. As André says, I have got inside Pascal. I don't have to make an effort to read Pascal, particularly the notes in the Brunschvicg edition that André gave me. Everything that relates to Port-Royal moves me.

Simon Duberc has passed his *bachot*, but has he read Pascal? I suspect him of knowing none of his set books by direct contact, but only through the medium of his manual . . . He was walking beside me. I was conscious of that smell of sweat in which his cassock is steeped. Not that he is dirty; he is cleaner than his peasant family, who don't know what washing means, and even perhaps than ourselves, since he's in the water almost every day, up at the mill pond where he goes fishing. He fishes for pike and dace by poking among the alder stumps, in front of which he has spread nets . . . But I don't propose to tell fishing stories.

Really, it's not so much Simon's smell that makes me feel sick as that sixth little finger he has on each hand, that quivering appendage, and a sixth toe on each foot, so that his made-to-measure shoes look as broad as they're long, like elephants' feet! But I seldom have an opportunity to see those sixth toes, whereas that bit of boneless gristle on each hand fascinates me. He does not try to hide it, moreover, and rejoices openly that his extra fingers have enabled him to dodge military service. His elder brother Prudent thinks otherwise: 'You could have got into Saint-Cyr . . .' That was the only time I have heard Prudent play the tempter towards his younger brother, although that's the role attributed to him by Mother and M. le Doyen.

I have thought of a novel I could write round this theme: Prudent, who is lean, puny and swarthy, and whose teeth are all rotten, and who, I know, loves Marie Duros, the girl next door, the sister of Adolphe Duros who is twenty and looks like the picture of Hercules in my Greek history book – Prudent might make use of his brother to be revenged on the world where he himself is a sort of mildew . . . Except that, like all the Dubercs, he is intelligent. His revolt shows that. In the story I am inventing, Prudent would give up Marie Duros and bring her and Simon together. Actually Marie Duros must loathe the younger brother just as much as the elder and indeed much more, because of those little fingers and the way his cassock must stick to his skin . . . What do I know about it? I've made that up, but I am sure it's true, because I know the boy that Marie loves, at least the boy she goes with, a friend of her brother, Adolphe the giant.

In any case M. le Doyen may not be so far wrong when he says: Simon's enemy is not the demon of lust but the demon of ambition.

He never looks at girls. I know he has been brought up not to look at them. All the same, it can't have been much of a struggle for him . . . What do I know about it? I know nothing about Simon or anyone else. Even Mother and M. le Doyen often puzzle me.

When we got back from shooting, Laurent took the hare into the kitchen. I was tired and I lay down on the couch in the hall. Mother came to sit beside me. She laid her hand on my forehead and asked me if I was thirsty. She seemed to want to talk to me. She must have settled with M. le Doyen what to say to me, because I was supposed to be in Simon's confidence. Actually this is not the case. His liking for me never takes the form of words. He is not embarrassed by the gulf between us; at any rate, he has never tried to cross it.

That's true of my mother too. She loves me, but she's not interested in me. She is interested in nothing but her estates and also something that she shares with nobody, religious scruples I imagine, of the sort that used to torment me myself when I was small, and from which I have been almost completely freed since I discovered, thanks to Donzac, that we have been trained to confine the infinite within ridiculous interdicts, graded into venial and so-called mortal sins.

Mother must have been commissioned by M. le Doyen to make me talk, and I deliberately kept my eyes closed, as if I was trying to sleep. She asked me, point blank, how Simon had behaved while we were out shooting.

'He was only thinking about the hare and probably about the black looks he'll get from M. le Doyen when he goes to serve at Mass tomorrow morning.'

Mother was ready for that, and she let me have it at one go.

'M. le Doyen is not so narrow-minded. He attaches no importance to the fact that Simon, at nineteen, prefers shooting to vespers. Sunday vespers are not obligatory. M. le Doyen told me that he found them a strain himself. In Simon's case, that's not where the harm lies.'

'No,' I said, 'the harm lies in dedicating him, possibly against his will, to a life for which he's not suited.'

Mother had what she calls a hot flush. She turned scarlet: what business was it of mine?

'But Maman, it was you who brought up the subject. I'm the one person, surely, who never interferes where Simon is concerned.'

With that utter lack of logic which is not peculiar to Mother but which, according to Donzac, is typical of all women, she protested that this was where I was in the wrong, and that I ought to have interfered.

'Don't you believe in Grace? Do you suppose God needs us in a conflict like this, which is going on inside Simon and concerns himself alone?'

'Simon has been subjected to pressures we never suspected, lately: a real plot. You've got to know, it's very serious: since the beginning of the holidays he's been secretly seeing a great deal of . . . guess who? The Mayor, yes, M. Duport, who's a Mason, a freethinker, and who has vowed to seduce him away from the Church . . .'

'But we all knew that Simon went to see Mme Duport . . .'

'Yes, that crazy creature, but not her husband, who goes mad when he sees a soutane. I used to believe that Simon only visited the Duports' house in the afternoon, when the mayor is at his saw-mill. It's been going on for a long time . . . Mme Duport warned us of it herself . . .'

Mme Duport herself! I couldn't believe my ears. 'We don't see the Duports.' In Mother's language, that means that she does not exchange with them the annual call, during the summer holidays at Maltaverne, of which three or four of the village ladies can boast. But it is also true literally: we don't see the Duports, we never look at them. They are obliterated from our tiny world. Now I shall try to straighten out this story of Simon and the Duports. Mme Duport, who was supposed to be pretty but always seemed old to me, is much younger than her husband ('nobody knows where he picked her up . . . where she came from . . .') and an object of suspicion because she's not from our part of the world, the *lande* of the Bazas region. The Duports had an only daughter, Thérèse, born the same day as Simon Duberc. Marie Duberc used to go to them as daily help, taking Simon along with her, and he played with Thérèse, let himself be bullied, and obeyed her as the charwoman's son was bound to obey the Mayor's daughter – but also, people said jokingly, because he was in love with her and she with him, and what she liked best about him was what I loathed myself, that sixth little finger . . . Thérèse died suddenly, after a few days' illness; was it meningitis? The parents had complete trust in Dr Dulac, the deputy Mayor, who was also a radical and a freemason. They were heart-broken. Mme Duport, who used to go to church on Sundays, stopped going, and turned against God. On the other hand she went to the church-yard every day and in all weathers. When cherries were in season she used to take some to Thérèse's grave because the child had been fond of them. The schoolchildren used to come and eat them up.

These eccentricities deterred one's pity. To crown it all she refused to see Mother. That was really unbelievable. In fact, nobody in our village set foot in her house any more, except for Marie Duberc and Simon during the holidays. We learnt through them that the rushes which had been strewn on the hall floor on the day of the funeral had been left lying there, and Marie Duberc had been forbidden to touch them.

As for Simon, Mme Duport would have kept him with her day and night if she could. For her, he brought back Thérèse, he *was* Thérèse. But in fact he was alive, and a little boy; she could not put him down on a chair, like an object, nor stuff him with biscuits and preserves all day. Fortunately he was crazy about reading. I remember that later on, when we were playing a game in which you had to invent a motto that would express in the fewest possible words your conception of happiness, Simon had at first written 'shooting and reading', and then corrected this to 'reading and shooting'. Mme Duport had complete sets of the illustrated *Saint Nicolas* magazine, of the *Journal des Voyages*, of Jules Verne's novels, as well as *Le Tour de France de deux enfants* and many other wonderful things. She would settle Simon down in front of the window and say to him: 'Read, forget about me.'

To begin with Simon had been embarrassed by feeling her gaze fixed on him and by the click of her knitting needles, and then he became used to it; every two or three days, or even every day when his book was particularly enthralling, he would come and settle down in the afternoon beside the window of that room which must have been very odd, but which he was never able to describe to me: peasants may see what we do not, but they don't see what we see. One day he asked Mme Duport if he might take the book home. This was the only time she was ever cross with him. None of the books that Thérèse had read, that had been touched by Thérèse's hands might leave the house. But next day she told Simon she would like him to read aloud to her while she knitted, and that she would pay him by the hour like his mother.

I wonder whether it was these wages, which dazzled the Dubercs, that prevented Mother and M. le Doyen from being as concerned as they might have been at this daily contact between a twelve-year-old seminarist and the eccentric wife of the freethinking Mayor. It is true that at this period the Mayor was never at home, being fully occupied all day by his factory and by the administration of the commune. Moreover, as I learnt later, he had two mistresses, one at Bordeaux and the other at Bazas.

It was true that Mme Duport, who had been estranged from God since the death of Thérèse, no longer went to church, but Simon had assured the Doyen that she never spoke to him about religion. In fact she never spoke to him about anything, she just watched him reading. 'At first it used to worry me, as if she were gobbling me up with her eyes. But now I don't notice it . . .' Simon assured us. It did not even take away his appetite when she brought him his four o'clock snack of a slice of bread and butter and a big cup of cocoa, and stared at him all the time while he ate it.

In October, when we all returned to Bordeaux, Simon took the pocket money he had earned back to the seminary with him. Neither M. le Doyen nor Mother ever imagined that he ought to have given it up. It used to amaze me, even as a child, that for these Christian folk money should be something of such unquestionable value, something never to be sacrificed except in the case of a very special vocation, such as a Franciscan's or a Trappist's. By the time I was twelve I had begun to realize something that Donzac has made clear to me during these last two years – that the Christians who have brought us up take, unconsciously, the opposite line to the Gospel in everything, turning each of the Beatitudes in the Sermon on the Mount into a curse; that they are not meek, they are not merely unjust but they execrate justice.

What provoked the drama was the soutane they put on Simon when he turned fourteen. That soutane was a tremendous promotion. It entitled him to a surplice during Church services and a stall in the choir. And although the village people continued to *tutoyer* him, strangers addressed him as M. l'abbé in spite of his childish face. But a soutane in the Mayor's house! Mme Duport assumed that he'd be willing to unfrock himself twice a week. But he refused, as though his hopes of eternal salvation were at stake. Marie Duberc, for whom the soutane meant the realization of her lifelong dream – a presbytery where she would be in command of the kitchen and the wash-house – actually dared to approve of Simon's refusal.

Mother and M. le Doyen then got an inkling of what I, at fourteen, could see quite clearly, that what Mme Duport wanted was no longer the company of Thérèse's little friend, but of Simon Duberc just as he was, repellent as I found him, with his strong smell, his heavy peasant frame, and those extra fingers of his. It was obvious that she could not do without him; she would only accept his absence during the school terms, which must have seemed to her, I imagine, a sort of liturgical advent, a time of preparation for the coming of Simon . . . But no, as I remember now, neither my mother nor the Doyen suspected anything. What opened their eyes was a remark of Mme Duport's which Simon reported to the Doyen: that it was her husband who couldn't stand the sight of his cassock, whereas she was getting used to it and indeed could see its advantages, feeling sure that Simon would always be available, that nobody would take him from her . . .

'No other woman?' I asked.

'I suppose so,' Mother replied.

'Then she must be in love with him!'

I made this remark, drawing the obvious conclusion, in a completely matter-of-fact tone, and was astonished at the effect it produced. It is true that I was fourteen that year, but they treated me as an eight-year-old boy would not be treated nowadays.

'What are you saying? You're talking nonsense! You don't know what you're talking about.'

'The proof that I do know is that I'm talking about it.'

'You should be ashamed, at your age. What will M. le Doyen think of you?'

'Out of the mouths of babes and sucklings . . .' he said.

He stood up and began walking round the billiard table, muttering: 'How could I have been so blind? . . .'

'But M. le Doyen, you surely don't believe . . . At Mme Duport's age!'

'It's a dangerous age, unfortunately! . . . Of course, in my opinion Simon is quite safe: I know him . . .'

He stopped short, afraid of having said too much. What he knew of Simon, even the good he knew of him, belonged to the secret of the confessional.

'Yes,' I said, 'but according to Simon she never stops looking at him while he's eating his "four o'clock". Perhaps some day she's going to want more than that . . .'

'What are you trying to insinuate? But who's been teaching you . . .'

'It's quite true,' the Doyen said in a low voice, 'there are ogresses . . .'

'And ogres too,' I added innocently.

They were staring at me anxiously: what was I hinting at? Oh, no doubt I meant nothing very precise, or else I preferred not to talk about it, but I knew that ogres prowl round boys of fifteen; they only come close if they sense complicity.

'It's terrifying,' said Mother. 'Why does evil exist?' without knowing that she was asking the only question capable of defeating religious faith.

I am trying to remember what they thought up to protect Simon from this harpy. The curé got him invited to a shooting-party by one of his colleagues in the Charente, who kept him there until term began. That year Simon went back to his seminary without re-visiting Maltaverne.

As for me . . . Dare I remind myself of the trick I played on M. le Doyen? Yes, I must, if I'm to see myself clearly as I really am. On September 7, the eve of the Blessed Virgin's Nativity, Mother, without even giving herself time to beat about the bush, told me that M. le Doyen would expect me at three o'clock for confession: 'so you'll get your turn before the ladies'. It seemed quite natural to her

to interfere in the religious life of a fourteen-year-old boy. I was just
a child, and she held herself responsible for me in the sight of God.
Annoyed and irritated, but not furious as I should be today, I could
understand how her mind worked, since I have inherited her morbid
scruples and even now, at seventeen, I am not yet cured of them. She
must have been brooding over what I had ventured to say about
ogres: I should have to pour it all out to the priest. Not that there
was any question, for her, of violating the secret of the confessional:
Maman did not want to 'know'. She merely needed to be reassured
that her little boy had been 'taken in hand' as the dangerous age drew
near. I fought back: observance of the September Lady-Day had
ceased to be compulsory since the Concordat.

'In our family,' my mother said, 'it's still compulsory. We have
always kept it up. Our tenant farmers don't harness their oxen that
day. Besides, M. le Doyen is expecting you. There's no going back
on it.'

'But you don't force Laurent . . .'

'Laurent is eighteen. You are a child under my care.'

The devil inspired me: 'If I make a bad confession, I shall make a
bad communion, and you will be responsible for a double sacrilege.'

She turned pale, or rather ashen. I flung my arms round her neck:
'Of course I was joking, I'll confess and I'll take communion . . .'
She hugged me close.

On the way to church my rage flared up again, but this time
against the innocent priest. I tried to control it: I must not cheat at
confession . . . 'I'll tell him everything,' I said to myself, 'more than
he wants to hear and more than he's ever heard before.'

He was reading his breviary, sitting beside the confessional. He
went on reading for a few minutes, then he asked me if I was ready.
He went into his recess and unhooked the curtain. I heard the panel
slide back, and saw his enormous ear. I told him I had not been to

confession since August 15, hurried through the *Confiteor* and launched straight into my usual little catalogue, which had scarcely changed since my first confession: 'I accuse myself of greed, of telling lies, of disobedience, of laziness, of having said my prayers badly, of being inattentive at Mass, of pride, of slander . . .'

Was that all? He looked disappointed. Yes, I really thought that was all.

'You're sure there is nothing else worrying you? Even if it were only thoughts . . .'

'What kind of thoughts?' I asked him.

He did not insist. He was uneasy; I was a monster, but I might equally well be an innocent monster.

'Have you always confessed yourself sincerely?'

At that moment the devil got into me and prompted me to answer: 'No, Father.'

'What's that? I hope it was about nothing serious.'

'I don't know. Perhaps the most serious sin of all.'

'My poor child! Your mother, your teachers, and I myself have tried to put you on your guard against any lapse from the sacred path of virtue . . .'

He meant purity. I protested that I had nothing serious to confess on that head. It was true at the time. What an innocent little boy I was, three years ago . . .

'But you said it was the most serious sin of all . . . What does this mean?'

'You can judge for yourself whether it's serious or not. You see, I'm an idolater.'

'An idolater? What are you talking about?'

'There's something I adore, quite literally, and I daren't tell you . . . I worship secretly . . . you know the big oak tree in the park?'

'It's not so very big,' said the priest, in order, I suppose, to bring me back into the reassuring world where things can be weighed and measured.

'That is my God; yes, since I was old enough to think for myself, I have always worshipped it as a god.'

'Well, well! You are a poet, we all know.' (He pronounced it 'powet'.) 'There's no harm in that.'

'I knew you wouldn't believe me, Father. That's what has prevented me until now from confessing my sin: the certain knowledge that nobody would believe me, not even you. But how can I make you understand that I have made up a liturgy in honour of the big oak tree, that I offer up sacrifices to it . . .'

'Come now, come now! That's all harmless powetry, my poor boy. What are you thinking of? unless you're trying to make a fool of me. That would really be a serious sin: you can't make fun of God.'

'I'm not making fun of you but I realize you cannot believe me.'

'All poets, even Christian ones, adore Nature, that's not forbidden.'

'What I feel has nothing to do with the outpourings of Lamartine or Hugo. Of course all trees are alive and divine for me, especially the pine trees in the park. I love them better than men,' I added, overcome by an excitement that was both contrived and sincere, and to which I yielded with rapture.

Yes, I was already afraid of men, even the men-to-be who were my school-fellows. Our religious teachers, even the worst of them, did not really frighten me because they are restrained by piety and discipline. But my schoolfellows! They were capable of anything, already! I remember spending the whole of break, one day, shut up in the lavatory because I was terrified of having a ball thrown at me at close range.

'Come now, Alain, let's get back to serious matters.'

'Why do you deny me forgiveness,' I asked in genuine, if

selfconscious and self-indulgent distress, 'by refusing to take my confession seriously?'

The priest was pulling at his face as though kneading a lump of clay, a characteristic gesture of his. He suddenly asked me:

'Do you worship all trees and not only the big oak tree?'

'No, they're all living creatures of course, but only the big oak is God.'

'Have you had a revelation of this?'

I could see him shaking his big head, not daring to touch his forehead with his forefinger.

'No, there's never been any revelation. As far back as I can remember I've always worshipped the earth and the trees . . .'

'Not animals? That's something to be thankful for.'

'No, not animals . . . Oh yes, though! I'd quite forgotten,' I said, 'but it's all coming back to me. You know the deserted farm, Father?'

'The one at Silhet?'

'When I was seven or eight years old, somebody or something put it into my head that our old donkey, Grisette, who had died of old age a few months before, was inside that deserted farm. I convinced myself of it and I persuaded Laurent to believe it, although he was older than I was. It was only a game for him, but not for me. We used to go to the deserted farm and sing a sort of nonsense chant in front of the locked door: "Grisette, Grisette, happy birthday to you, I'll give you some preserved apricots" . . .'

'Preserved apricots, for a donkey?' The curé forced himself to laugh, as though to restore things to their right proportions.

'It was because when I was seven I could think of nothing better in the world than preserved apricots, but I literally did worship Grisette. I've suddenly realized, Father, that I was actually committing the abominable sin of which the heathen accused the early Christians, the worship of a donkey's head.'

I stopped talking, genuinely appalled by what I had just discovered, and the curé was silent too, perhaps wondering whether he
should turn me out of the confessional for making fun of him. But
how could one tell? – was I really making fun of him? He knew
from experience that I had been a sensitive child, subject to the same
morbid scruples as my mother. He suddenly asked me out loud, in
an almost solemn tone:

'Alain, do you believe in God?'

'Oh yes, Father!'

'Do you believe that Jesus is the Christ, the son of the living God,
that He gave His life for you, and rose again from the dead?'

I believed it with all my heart and with all my mind.

'Do you love the Holy Virgin?'

'Yes, I love her . . .'

'Then stop thinking about all that nonsense. If you've sinned,
I shall absolve you, or rather the Lord Himself will absolve
you.'

He hurried off to the sacristy, as though making his escape. I
barely took time to say my penance, and then I was outside in the
drowsy heat of early September. A mild breeze was blowing, a mere
breath: that poetic cliché was true enough today: the breath of a
living being. I had meant to play a trick on the Doyen, and now I
discovered that this trick had brought me not release from, but
awareness of a love which remained my constant refuge. This was a
worship which had never encroached upon that other love, that
other worship which I had vowed to the Christian God, identified
with the bread and wine that are born from the earth, the sun and
the rains. I needed this twofold refuge; I should never have too
many refuges from men. Two years have gone by since then, and
my anguish grows greater daily, the nearer I come to that which
seems to me horrible beyond all other horrors: life in an army

barracks. I've admitted this to no one, not even Donzac. I am not ashamed of my anguish, I know it's not despicable, provided one does not give it form by expressing it: then it would become cowardice. I sometimes think, as if it were my last resort, that perhaps I may die before I go before the Medical Board.

At the same time that I was thinking about these things on the way home, I kept remembering how the Doyen had faced up to the trap I had set him. And although he was among the first in the list of stupid Catholics that Donzac and I had drawn up, with a parallel list of intelligent Catholics, I marvelled at the way he had dealt with it, showing a tact that he never had in ordinary life, as though he had been momentarily inspired. That he was inspired I had no doubt. At heart I was not at all convinced of my own innocence as to the sin of idolatry, and while confessing it I had come to believe in it. Otherwise, my relief would not have shown itself in a mad race round the park, in which I made Laurent join me. I can always beat him at running, although he is four years older, because he soon gets out of breath.

What sort of communion I made next day I cannot remember. One forgets one's communions as easily as one's dreams. And yet I have a clear recollection of that day, September 8, three years ago. I refused to join Laurent shooting larks in Jouanhaut's field. I remember the violent feeling I had that day, because it is something I often feel even now: the desire to be alone, to walk through woods and fields, to go on to the point of exhaustion along those sandy paths where I should never meet a soul except some tenant leading his oxen, who'd touch his beret and greet me with an *Aduchats*, or else a shepherd with his flock. In that faceless heath there'd be nobody to stare at me. And yet I had made up my mind to go and see somebody. Of the three or four objects for walks between which I generally hesitated – the source of the Hure, the great pine tree (a

giant that draws visitors from miles around) and the old fellow of
Lassus, it was the old man that I chose, maybe because he was over
eighty and would not be much longer at Lassus, which he had
refused to leave all his life. He had not been out shooting for many
years, except for woodpigeon in October. How did he spend his
days? He had looked astonished when I told him one day that there
were people crazy enough to buy books. He saw nobody except the
doctor. He used to say that the curé might get him dead but wouldn't
have him alive. As for his heirs (he was related to all the landed
gentry of the neighbourhood and was even a distant cousin of our
own), he used to set the dogs on to any one of them who tried to
come near him. They would joke about it together, knowing that he
hated them all equally. Their only hope lay in that terror of death
which, according to the notary, had prevented old Lassus from
making his will. But Seconde, who took care of him after having
slept with him for over forty years, must have seen to it that he did
what was needed. She would surely inherit his eight hundred
hectares, or rather her son Casimir would inherit them, for she was
under the thumb of that lout who had never done anything in his
life but shoot woodpigeon for old Lassus in October. The rest of the
year he did odd jobs when he wasn't drunk, drew water from the
well, sawed wood. I might see him or I might not: I didn't care. He
belonged to the world of things rather than of people, like the big
pine tree, like the old man of Lassus himself. There was nothing
human about them, in the terrifying sense of the word. Brutes as
they were, they did not belong to that species of which I was
frightened, from which I was eager to escape.

I went on walking. The bracken was not yet touched by autumn:
it was nearly as tall as I was in those days, for I have only grown
during the past year. The bracken was my enemy because I had been
told, ever since my childhood, that it contained prussic acid. I
struck off the heads of the proudest ferns and now and then I flung

myself into the dense clusters and breathed in their noxious sap as though it were blood I had shed.

As I passed by Silhet, the deserted farm where I had worshipped Grisette, I heard the sound of galloping hooves drawing near and I barely had time to stand aside: Mlle Martineau rode past without seeing me, or at any rate without condescending to see me, astride like Joan of Arc, and her fair curls streaming in the wind seemed alive, like living serpents growing out of her. Perhaps she had been afraid I might cut her. Although we were cousins, and the Martineaus were connected with 'all the best families in the region', as Mother said, we did not 'see them' either, for our family had quarrelled with the Martineaus many generations ago. Our grandfathers had not been on speaking terms. But Mlle Martineau was subject to a special ostracism – for reasons which at that time (I'm better informed nowadays) I attributed to the impropriety of not riding side-saddle, added to the fact that she worked for her living, as companion and reader to the baronne de Goth, at Bazas – a person who was not one of us, who belonged to a different sphere, Mother said, with whom we could have no possible contact, whose private life, unlike the lives of people in our set, was not answerable to any final judgment, any more than the behaviour of ants, raccoons or badgers: 'that baronne de Goth', Mother would begin, 'they say that she . . . But you wouldn't understand!'

I have never seen Mlle Martineau except on her horse: she is as firmly fixed to it, in my mind, as my lead soldiers on their mounts. Since she lives at Bazas she is never to be seen at Mass or at any funeral . . .

The old man's house was fenced off from the farm. Some puny dahlias grew in the garden plot, which was tended by Seconde; she appeared on the doorstep as soon as the dogs began barking at my approach. The old man shouted from inside: '*Quezaco?*' She shaded

her eyes with her hand, and on recognizing me called back towards
the half-open door: *'Lou Tchikoi de lou Prat!'* To the old man, I was
'the lad from Lou Prat', because the wood where my grandfather
had had his house built had been called Lou Prat and went by that
name until the day, not so long ago, when Laurent and I had
changed its name because there was a very stupid fat boy at school
called Louprat. It was I who had insisted on the name Maltaverne,
the title of a story which had delighted me in a number of the
St Nicholas magazine of the 'nineties; but the old man of Lassus
knew it only as Lou Prat.

Seconde's hair was hidden by a black kerchief; her lips were
sucked in by the dreadful emptiness of her mouth. Then the old man
appeared, shaggy and unshaven, wearing a torn and faded cardigan
and woollen slippers, in spite of the heat. He professed not to know
his age, but he had served in the ranks of the Versaillais during the
Commune, and for him Paris still meant the Communards. He never
talked about this to anyone except Laurent and myself, who did not
belong to the hated company of his heirs – to myself particularly, for
he was fond of me, I could sense that, just as Simon Duberc is, or the
abbé Grillot, who used to give me half marks even when I failed my
exams.

'He's growing, he's growing! We shall have to put a stone on his
head.'

There followed an argument between the old man and Seconde. I
don't speak patois but I understand it. The old man was ordering
her to bring a bottle of beer. Seconde stared at me with her sharp
bird's eyes and protested that he had drunk enough beer, that it
would give him a chill on the stomach. Even though I wasn't one
of the heirs, you could never be sure ... She had to give way,
however, and she set the bottle and glasses on a rusty garden table.
As she remained standing close behind us the old man shouted to
her: *'A l'oustaou!'* (Get back into the house!) She obeyed, but she

must have stayed listening between the half-open shutters of the kitchen.

The old man and I clinked glasses. He fixed his eighty-year-old gaze on me, undisturbed by the silence between us . . . With a certain vague nostalgia, maybe? No, it's stupid to use the word 'nostalgia' of that ancient wild boar of a man, who had lived his eighty years of life like a single day, always the same day, with his gun within reach and his bottle of Médoc at every meal, the only visible sign of his wealth: as grimy in appearance, as ignorant as the grimiest and most ignorant of the tenant farmers whom he terrified. And yet his first words did betray a kind of nostalgia.

'I was at Bordeaux in '93, I stayed there three days, at the Hotel Montré. There was a bath-tub . . .'

'Did you use it?'

'To catch my death? No thanks!'

He was silent, and then suddenly: 'I used to eat over the way, at the "Chapon fin". The wines they have there . . .' He fell silent again and then began to snigger. I averted my eyes so as not to see the two stumps of teeth he still had left in front. He asked me: 'D'you know the Château Trompette?'

'But Monsieur Dupuy, it was pulled down over a hundred years ago!'

'It wasn't pulled down in '93, because I went there.' He couldn't stop laughing. The Château Trompette was a brothel, and the 'bad boys' at school used to talk about it in the corner of the playground.

'Costs a lot . . . Not your sort of place yet.'

I suddenly felt convinced, at that minute, that only a small number of souls are destined for immortality and that hell, for those who are not chosen, is nothingness. Moreover the Lord has only promised immortality to a few: 'and the life of the world to come.' And again: 'he who eats of this bread shall not die.' But the rest will.

I had no doubt but that this was one of those lightning-flash intuitions which André Donzac used to say were a special grace, which
he admired in me, and which made up for my not having a philo-
sophical turn of mind. (I wrote that very evening to tell him what I
had discovered about the immortality of the few; I thought I should
impress him, but he replied by return of post making fun of my
ridiculous notion: 'all souls are immortal, or else none are.') I thus
reflected, with exquisite relish, that there would be nothing left of
the old man, or Seconde, or Casimir, not even enough to feed the
feeblest flicker of hell fire.

'You're not old enough yet . . .'

He must have felt vaguely remorseful for having mentioned
Château Trompette, for he changed the subject abruptly and wanted
to know what they were saying about him in the village.

'They're still wondering whether you've signed a certain paper . . .'

I had dropped my voice because of Seconde, who must have been
listening.

'They're wondering whether Seconde and Casimir are going to
carry off the prize, or whether they've already done so . . .'

I was touching on the forbidden subject. The old man glared at
me resentfully: 'And what do you think?'

'Oh, if I was one of your heirs, I shouldn't worry!'

'Why's that?'

I knew what to say to the old man to drive him wild.

'Better not talk; Seconde is listening.'

'She's deaf, you know that.'

'She can hear when she wants to, you told me so yourself.'

He insisted. I felt he was uneasy, disturbed. Donzac says I am a
disturbing person, in the absolute sense. Not always; but that day I
was.

'It's impossible that, shrewd as you are, Monsieur Dupuy, you
shouldn't have understood that so long as you haven't signed that

paper, it's to the interest of Seconde and Casimir that you shouldn't die.'

He growled: 'Don't talk about that!'

'But that's the whole crux of the matter. The day you've signed, it'll be just the opposite: their interest will lie . . .'

He interrupted me with a kind of moan like a dog baying. 'I tell you don't talk about that.'

He got up, took a few steps, dragging his gouty foot. He turned round and shouted to me: *'Bey-t'en!'* (Off with you!)

'I didn't mean to offend you, Monsieur Dupuy.'

'They're not murderers, after all: they're attached to me.'

I nodded, with a sneering laugh that mimicked his own. 'Of course, because they're bloodsuckers; and they're too much afraid to become murderers. If you've signed the paper, they know they'd be the first to be suspected in case of anything fishy about your death, and that your heirs would carry on a relentless inquiry. All the same . . .'

I had crossed to the other side of the yard; the old man stood there among the dahlias, profoundly upset because I had spoken to him of his death, even more than by the threat of murder. 'What? what?' he was muttering. He had turned sickly pale, as though death had struck him already. I might have been the murderer myself. I did not think of that. I plunged on, seized by a sort of fury.

'All the same, Monsieur Dupuy, and you must have thought of it yourself, in a place as lonely as Lassus, where there's no danger of witnesses, it wouldn't be hard, you must admit, to get rid of somebody, without running the slightest risk . . .'

'Bey-t'en!'

'I'm not sure,' I went on, reflectively, as though talking to myself, 'if an autopsy would show when someone had been smothered under an eiderdown. And then there's the inevitable bronchopneumonia when an old man is strapped naked to his bed the whole of a winter's night in front of an open window, provided the temperature is several degrees below zero! There again, I don't know whether the autopsy . . .'

'Get out, or I'll call Casimir.'

Casimir was at that very moment coming out of the farm. I fled without turning round to cast a last glance at Lassus, knowing very well I'd never go back there as long as the old man was alive . . .

Well, none of that is true. It was a story I made up for myself. It's all untrue, from where the old man told me about Château Trompette. Pure fiction! – is it well done or badly? – in any case it rings false. The old man would never have let me get the words out. Besides, I would never have committed the mortal sin of accusing Casimir and Seconde of murder, or intent to murder; in fact, they are genuinely attached to their old bully. And then there's another version of the story, in which the old man suddenly decides that I am to be his heir. I imagine all I could do with the money; I would turn Lassus into a library, and Donzac and I would keep all our books there and we'd share them, segregated from the world of the living by a vast collection of books, and by music too, there would be a piano for André, and why not an organ?

Did I tell myself this story on the way home? I remember nothing, except that I was peaceful and happy as I almost always am when I've taken communion that morning. I thought how my adolescence was being spent in a world of monsters, or rather caricatures of monsters, some of whom were fond of me and others afraid of me. I'd never yet had a girl come to me, as they do in stories, although at school they say I'm nice-looking, but I'm thin and have no muscles. André says girls don't like boys that are too thin. The only girl I admire I only see on horseback: as inaccessible as Joan of Arc. She despises me too much even to look at me. Yes . . . but that's what attracts me about her, that it's quite safe and she'll not get off her

horse and she'll not come to me to force me to give up being a child
and behave like a man . . . Did I think of that on the way back from
Lassus? Or is it yet another story I'm inventing? There are other
girls who disturb me: those that sing in the church choir, gathered
round Sœur Lodoïs at the harmonium . . . Especially the chemist's
daughters, who wear black velvet ribbons round necks curved like
ring-doves' . . .

During those holidays, nothing happened out of the ordinary
course of our circumscribed life. Simon was no longer there. Nobody talked much about Mme Duport; there was a rumour that she
had taken to drink, and according to Marie Duberc, who still went
charring there, she even 'got up in the night to drink'. The Duport–
Simon trail was lost among many others; then the autumn term
began, and we went back to Bordeaux; Maltaverne became the
enchanted island which I dreamed about till the next summer
holidays, the ones before I moved up into the *classe de rhétorique*. The
only thing that happened was that the Mayor stopped objecting to
Simon's visiting them in his soutane. Mother and the Doyen re-
joiced, as though this were a victory, or at least they pretended to
rejoice. Had M. Duport already begun to see Simon in secret? – had
he started trying to wean him from the Church? According to
Simon, when they met, the Mayor never talked to him of religion
but was just very friendly, sometimes asking his advice on one subject or another, or talking about the political friends he met at the
General Council. He was indeed on very good terms with the young
minister Gaston Doumergue: he could get anything he wanted from
him . . .

That year, Simon was very reticent about the Mayor. Then came
the thunderbolt of Mme Duport's visit to the sacristy after Mass, to
tell the Doyen about her husband's plot. According to Mother, the
Mayor had promised Simon he would support him until he had

passed his *licence*, and even after that, if he was willing to work for the École Normale and the Agrégation.

It was impossible, Mme Duport said, to make out Simon's reactions. She thought he was tempted, but hesitant. The Doyen was afraid of ruining everything by interfering. I had made him conscious of his clumsiness. I saw this quite clearly on this occasion, and moreover that he depended on me to disentangle the confusion in the mind and heart of a peasant boy turned seminarist, who had suddenly become the stake, at village level, in the battle being waged throughout France between Church and State – or rather between the Religious Orders and Freemasonry.

I knew that Simon would elude the conflict even before it began. He must have a friend at the Seminary in whom he confides everything; I myself am a superior being as far as he's concerned, I am Madame's son; he loves me, that's true, but I'm as inaccessible in his eyes as Mlle Martineau or the pole-star are for me. He'll say nothing, unless . . .

I have always found it easier to write than to speak: pen in hand, nothing stops me. I've thought of a letter I could send Simon, I told M. le Doyen.

'But he knows more theology than you do!'

'It's not a question of theology! I know what line I shall take to attack him . . .'

In point of fact I had only thought of it two minutes before and it was still very nebulous, but I had begun to see my way.

The Doyen insisted: 'Make him talk!'

'As I keep telling you, he'll say nothing to me. In any case, no one ever says anything to anyone else. I wonder if there are actually some people who express their thoughts with questions and answers like they do in novels and plays . . .'

'Whatever do you mean? Surely that's what we do all day long; what we're doing at this moment?'

'True enough, monsieur le curé, but how often do you and I have even a fragmentary conversation like this one? Between Mother and myself, as far as I can remember, talk has consisted of general comments, often in patois, since they have to do for the farm people and the servants too. Perhaps people are divided by differences of age or social class to such an extent that there is no common language . . . But I've noticed that the farm people don't talk amongst themselves either; when they meet they ask each other: *'As dejeunat?'* (Have you had lunch?) Their most important, indeed their only interest in life is the food that they may or may not have chewed with their toothless gums, like ruminants. When people love each other, do they talk about it?' I sighed. The curé repeated: 'Whatever do you mean?'

'If Mother were here she'd add: "what nonsense you talk!" And that would be the end of it . . . But one can always write. I can write a fine letter to Simon, and he'll read it and re-read it and keep it close to his heart . . .'

'You're crazy with pride,' the Doyen said. 'What do you think you are?' And after a silence: 'What are you going to write to him? You don't even know,' he insisted.

'I know what direction I want to take, or rather I've got to take . . . It's not what I want myself.'

I had only meant to tease M. le Doyen, and yet I couldn't help being excited by my own idea. What I meant to write to Simon was taking shape before my inward eye. I couldn't wait to write it down, to be sure that something so wonderful should not be wasted.

II

After over a year, I have gone back to this notebook; I broke off not for lack of matter, heaven knows, but because what I lived through defied all comment and above all was the end of my childish self. No, that's not true; I have become someone different and yet I'm still the same. I can't get over what I wrote when I was seventeen. Now, today, I'm entering on my nineteenth year, and certainly of my own accord I would put down nothing of what I have experienced. But Donzac attaches great importance – absurdly, to my mind – to my reactions to everyday life. . . . No, it's not absurd. The basis of it all is that Donzac, who is infinitely more intelligent than I am (although he wrote to me: 'you're not quite as intelligent as myself, but nearly . . .') is sterile to a point that he himself finds astonishing: he can understand everything but express nothing. He doesn't compose, he doesn't create. But that's not all: he cannot set forth anything; he's capable of startling phrases, but not of any sort of development. It was always my essay that had the honour of being read out loud in class, never his. He found this more extraordinary than I did: 'when I think that it's you and not me!' he would sigh, 'that it's you who will become somebody, whereas I shall be nobody till my dying day!' But that's just what is marvellous about him; he has never considered this unfair. He believes that I shall be a writer and even a great writer, while he will spend all his life teaching the rudiments of knowledge to ignorant seminarists. But he also believes that, starting from anything I may write on a given subject, based on my own experience of life, he, André Donzac, will be capable of something beyond my powers, of

29

what he calls 'discovering'. Discovering what? What he's trying to
do is to shed light on the secret point where the truth of life
as we experience it joins revealed truth – the revealed truth
that has to be extracted from the matrix that has hardened round
the word of God through the Church's two thousand years of
history. . . .

And so it was decided between us that I should set down in black
and white, without missing out a single detail, everything that
happened at Maltaverne, and let him and nobody else into the secret
of it, tell the horrible story of Simon as it took shape within me, as it
still goes on working within me and tormenting me inwardly. I
realize that nothing can die within me and that I'm already encumbered with a whole dark, wretched world of thoughts. . . .
What will it be like when I have 'more memories than if I were a
thousand years old', as Baudelaire says? What a monstrous condition my old age will be! That's what makes me believe that I shall
die young. . . . No! That's not true: I don't believe I shall die young,
I don't believe I shall ever die, I feel incredibly eternal.

So this is how it all happened after my talk with the curé and the
promise I made him to speak to Simon, to overcome his silence by
means of a letter the essential lines of which were already in my
mind and which it would be impossible for him not to answer.

I went down towards the Hure, which is the stream that runs
through Maltaverne and where I knew Simon was fishing. It was
four o'clock, and I had taken a bunch of grapes from the kitchen as
I went through. The grass was a bit wet because the meadow was
once a marsh. I noticed that the hedge of alders (which people round
here call *vergnes*) looked blue. The grasshoppers and crickets that I
startled, the warm marshy smell, the sound of M. Duport's saw-mill,
a clatter of carts on the Sore road, all the sensations I experienced at

that moment are still with me: I shall never get rid of them as long as I live.

I could not see Simon at the far end of the meadow, but I could hear him. Hidden among the *vergnes*, I sat down by the waterside, knowing that since he was following the Hure upstream, striking the tree-stumps to drive out the pike and dace, he would eventually come to where I was and wouldn't be able not to speak to me. And then the match would begin.

The place where I was sitting was a carpet of mint. Dragonflies, blue and tawny, were flying round the flowering ferns. A day in the holidays, a September day, when I might have been spending my time like other boys of eighteen. . . . But actually, how do they spend their time? I daren't even pause to think about it. As for myself, at that moment, what devil or what angel was driving me? Was I acting a part, and if so who was prompting me? Who was making me rehearse my role before going on stage?

I could hear, at regular intervals, the splash as Simon took a step forward in the water, and suddenly I caught sight of him between a couple of alders: he was in bathing trunks, horribly white – the sort of white nakedness that I always find repulsive, with his solid peasant frame atrophied, as it were, by the intellectual life that had been imposed on the poor clodhopper. Unless perhaps it was the visible signs of his virility, the sight of his hairy maleness that repelled me? But I never linger over questions of this sort, having been accustomed from childhood to consider them 'bad thoughts'.

When Simon drew level with me I shouted to him: '*Aduchats!*' He turned round, exclaimed: 'Oh, I'm sorry!' jumped on to the bank and hurriedly pulled on trousers and a jersey over his wet trunks. He had not got his cassock, which surprised me. I told him to go on fishing. He said he'd finished, there was nothing there. The village people came very early to lift their nets. He kept glancing briefly at me and then averting his eyes, being at the same time eager to get away and – I'm daring to write it because it's true, and because nobody will ever read it except Donzac – under my spell; it was vital that he should be under my spell at that moment and that I should myself be in a state of 'lightning-flash intuition'. In point of fact Simon only wanted to escape, to escape from me. I had to detain him by force. I told him he had been setting people's tongues wagging lately. He scowled.

'People are talking? That don't matter to me. Oh, bugger!'

He must indeed have been upset to have spoken incorrectly and then to have used a swear-word in front of me! and above all to have repeated it: 'oh, bugger!' It's true that his brother Prudent punctuated every sentence with the word 'bugger' and that during his holidays I heard it all day. I protested that anything that happened to him did matter to me. Then he said, speaking insolently for the first time in his life, perhaps, to one of Madame's sons:

'It's my business, it's none of yours.'

'It's mine too, because I'm fond of you.'

He shrugged his shoulders and sneered. 'Was it the Doyen who told you to get me to talk, to worm things out of me?'

'You're very much mistaken if you think I'm on the side of the Doyen and Madame.'

'But you're surely not a friend of M. le Maire?'

'No, to be sure, but if I were in your place, if I could play your hand, I'd play it for all I was worth against both the Mayor and the curé.'

'Yes, but since nobody's asked you to do so. . . . But look here; what can you know, at eighteen, about what other people don't?'

'I know just what they don't know; I'm the only one that knows it.'

'Good Lord!' Simon had stopped in the middle of the field and was staring at me. 'You've got a cheek!'

'I know what I know, and you know that I know it.'

'What do I know?'

'That I'm the only person at Maltaverne who isn't blind, besides yourself; but you're too much involved to see things clearly, too deeply committed.'

'Well, have it your own way, Monsieur Alain. But you can bloody well leave me alone.'

The first time he'd ever been rude to me . . .

'Poor Simon! you're in a bad way; but I could help you to see clearly, with a single word . . . no, I'm boasting; you'd have to let me talk to you . . .'

'I don't want you to talk to me.'

'Then let me write to you. You don't mind my writing to you?'

'You never did so, not even when I took minor orders,' he said with sudden bitterness, 'not even when I got the prize for excellence. . . . Do I matter at all to you?'

'You know you do, Simon, you can't not know it, now that I'm so distressed on your account . . .'

'Oh, indeed! but what am I for you? Simon the peasant's son, whom everyone calls *tu* . . .'

'Except me.'

'Yes, that's true, except you, but I've always been Simon to you and you Monsieur Alain to me, even when you were four years old. Monsieur Laurent, Monsieur Alain! No, but really! Oh, bugger!'

He was beside himself. He was walking faster; I had almost to run to keep up with him. I insisted that he must let me write to him.

'What right have I to prevent you?'

'But promise me too that you'll read my letter.'

This time I must have hit on the right note. He stopped, we had reached the place where the meadow bends round. The shadows of the poplars had lengthened. It must have been five o'clock. Simon said: 'Yes, Monsieur Alain, I'll read your letter, I'll answer it. Calm down. But what can you know about me that other people don't?'

'One thing I can tell you right away, not from myself but from the Lord . . .'

He could only mutter: 'Well, for Heaven's sake!' I was playing for high stakes. My strength lay precisely in the fact that I was not playing: I was really inspired.

'These idiots don't know that the Lord loves you for what you are, namely an ambitious young man. There's no part of yourself that isn't loved, so why not the ambitious side of you?'

Although not a muscle of his face moved, I felt his attention on me. I pressed on: 'They're all equally blind. What we know, you and I, Simon, is that even though the Church seems to be that obsolete, run-down apparatus that the Mayor despises and that Mother and the Doyen confuse with the truth, you and I know that through that old-fashioned pipe-line there still flows, not profusely, sparingly indeed yet undeniably, the message of eternal life . . .'

I was spouting pure Donzac without being aware of it. Simon muttered: 'Well, for Heaven's sake! what's all that to do with ambition? You don't know what they've proposed to me. You yourself talked about an old-fashioned pipe-line . . . you know that life, the truth of life, doesn't flow through it any longer.'

'No, at heart I don't agree with what I said to you about an old-fashioned pipe-line, because the Church of Rome, its liturgy, its doctrine, even its history, with all its crimes and all its holiness, and then its art as embodied in our cathedrals, in the Gregorian chant, in Fra Angelico, is the most beautiful thing in the world – whereas what M. Loubet and M. Combe and the Paris law-courts stand for seems to me just about the meanest period in human history . . . But that's not the point. What's at stake is Simon Duberc, his destiny on earth and at the same time his eternal destiny. Now listen carefully: whatever glittering future is held out to you by M. Duport, that provincial freemason, even if it's a privileged place under Senator Monis, or even in Paris under Gaston Doumergue . . .'

'How do you know?'

How did I know? I had struck it lucky, not purely by chance: Doumergue had come to inaugurate our Agricultural Fair the previous year and M. Duport had introduced Simon to him.

'I know what the Lord allows me to know. But listen carefully: in secular life, whatever you do you'll be more or less made use of by party politicians, but without an outstanding gift of eloquence which you haven't got, you'll remain a subordinate, you'll never achieve anything worth while, you'll always lack something. . . .'

I hesitated; I was afraid of offending him. The only phrase that occurred to me was Mother's favourite expression, 'breeding'. Simon guessed my thoughts.

'Well, yes! I shall always be a peasant, a lout, and a spoiled priest into the bargain.'

'That's not what I meant to say, but think of this: a soutane changes a man, socially as well as spiritually. A soutane means a different skin. The field-marshal's baton in the private's haversack is just eyewash; but on the other hand the cardinal's hat hanging within reach of an intelligent little seminarist really exists, believe me, and it's up to you to take hold of it. Yes, everything depends on your willpower and intelligence. And that wouldn't prevent you from being a good priest, faithful to the duties of your calling, even a holy priest. There have been plenty of holy bishops and even holy cardinals.'

That was a stroke of genius! I had conferred sanctity on the highest position to which Simon aspired. He shook his head: 'That's all ancient history, it's over and done with, that chapter is closed. Combe has sounded the Church's death-knell . . .'

'Nonsense! The Church, which rules over five hundred million souls, will stand fast in spite of what's been happening in its province of France where the clergy, regular as well as secular, have behaved idiotically and walked straight into all the traps set by politicians of the nationalist right wing, and the faithful, like Panurge's sheep, have followed them . . .'

'Aha! you admit that we have been in the wrong?'

'Very much in the wrong, of course, and the word seems to me inadequate, because the Church's complicity with the forgers on the General Staff in order to keep an innocent man in a convict prison is something unpardonable, and she will have to pay the full price for it.'

Simon gaped at me. 'So you recognize that Dreyfus is innocent? Well, for Heaven's sake!'

'But Simon, I recognize what's obvious to anyone: that Combe's stupid anticlericalism exactly matches the stupid clericalism that has prevailed, and still prevails, on our side; we can study it here at home, in our own village, like a drop of water seen through a microscope: the way my mother acts towards her tenant-farmers, making them send their daughters to the convent school, while the lay schoolmistress is treated like a pariah, kept in the far corner of the church . . .'

Simon was mumbling: 'But then . . .'

'But then what? The fact that there's not an ounce of authentic Christianity in these professing Christians, and that we should treat them as they deserve, here and now, doesn't in any way affect the problem facing a young abbé who wants to rise to the top of the tree. What you need is to take the right direction from the start, to head for Paris, for the Catholic Institute, then if possible for Rome. The important thing is to become indispensable to one of the men who are active and prominent in the Church and who invariably need someone like yourself by their side, someone with "a head that can take everything in", as Mother says. They're not brilliant, for the most part.'

'I'm not brilliant myself.'

'Pooh! What matters is having "a head that can take things in".

You're well grounded, I imagine? a general knowledge of Thomism, what Donzac calls an unshakeable Thomism . . .'

We had halted in the middle of the field, facing the house. Simon had his back turned to it and did not see two black shapes, Mother and the Doyen, come out on to the terrace. As soon as they caught sight of us they went indoors hurriedly.

'Of course, Simon, you'll have to be familiar with the modernist errors that you'll have to combat. Have you read anything at all of Newman, Maurice Blondel, Le Roy, Loisy, Laberthonnière . . .'

He admitted piteously that he scarcely knew their names.

'Donzac will soon provide you with a reading list.'

'But he admires them?'

'Yes, but he often marvels at the stupidity and ignorance of their opponents, and he knows what arguments should be brought against them from the Thomist point of view. He'll easily enable you to fight them without appearing a reactionary. Anyhow, theology is the fundamental thing; it's important to choose your special subject, Canon law for instance, or some such branch of learning about which I'd be quite incapable of telling you anything; I haven't your sort of head, I can only take in certain things.'

I took the path that leads to the big oak tree so as not to risk being seen from the house again. It was hardly dusk yet, but we felt the coolness of the stream. Simon no longer sought to avoid me. I had gained that much at any rate. He walked with his eyes downcast, in a state of concentration that made him look as if he were made of stone: the hardness of that pallid, bloodless, lipless face, darkened with a two days' growth of beard, dwells in my mind's eye when I think of Simon. That's how he was looking as we drew near the big oak tree. He muttered: 'It's too late, too late!'

'It's not too late, since you're still there.'

I sat down on the bench, against the tree. He stood there. I thought I saw the wings of a big cockchafer flutter as it prepared to fly off. At all costs, I had to detain him.

I said: 'This big oak enabled me to play a trick on M. le Doyen.'

'Do you play tricks on M. le Doyen?'

I told him about my confession on September 7. He refused to believe me at first: 'Well, I never! For Heaven's sake!' He burst out laughing; I had never seen him laugh so heartily. Before initiating him into modernism we should teach him the use of a toothbrush.

'The cream of the joke,' I said, 'is that I really have practised that sort of idolatry ever since I was a child.'

I pressed my cheek against my beloved oak, and then, at great length, my lips. Simon sat down beside me. He had stopped laughing. He asked me: 'Was it a sacrilegious confession?'

'No, the Doyen decided not.'

'Was he thinking of other sins that you don't commit?'

I did not reply. Simon muttered: 'I'm sorry.'

'You needn't apologize, but I don't like talking about these things.'

'None the less they're connected with the whole business, with the whole argument. Yes, with what M. le Maire calls "the sin against nature" – compulsory celibacy . . . You can't know about that,' he said with sudden tenderness, 'you're an angel; at least half-demon, half-angel,' he added with a laugh.

'Listen to me, Simon, I know what it's all about, believe me. Of course a man must test himself before he consents to that pact, but if he has the strength and courage for it, what a help it will be towards his promotion! Think of the enormous advantage, when you set off on that upward journey, of not being encumbered with a family. Celibacy? Why, your best chance lies there.'

'Yes, but I'm talking about purity. If you heard M. Duport on the subject . . .'

'Is it any better to be like M. Duport, who keeps two mistresses and seduces his work girls?'

'Maybe not, but is it any worse?'

'The problem of the flesh, of the coexistence of the soul, which is capable of knowing God, with the most animal of instincts, has never in any case been solved by marriage.'

Simon murmured: 'All the same, some people love each other.'

'Yes, Simon, some people love each other. But perhaps that, too, is a vocation.'

'M. Duport says they've destroyed that in me, and in you too, at least so he supposes.'

'I've myself often laid the blame for that on the education we were given, my brother and I. But as it happens Laurent is like other boys. Indeed he was rather precocious about girls. Whereas I was born different . . . I was born squeamish . . . Not angelic, as you believe . . . But I'm going to surprise you: timid to the point of cowardice . . . There's a true incident at the bottom of all that. You know the fair they hold in Bordeaux on the Quincunxes, in October and March?'

'Oh, for heaven's sake, d'you think they take us seminarists to the fair?'

'It's a unique place, full of amazing poetry.'

'What? The Bordeaux fair?'

A peasant's first reaction is to think you're fooling him.

'Yes, every booth promises you some extraordinary sight. Each has its own private music and ignores all the rest; this creates a strange cacophony, interfused with the smell of toffee and fried potatoes – and it has its shady side, a woman's name over a minute booth, and the Fat Lady's arm or thigh suddenly showing through a hole in the canvas, and those paintings that show ladies and gentlemen tossing off champagne and the waiter, in evening dress, with a skull for a head – he is Death. And as a background there's the river, and a boat drifting past against the sky . . .'

'Why are you telling me this?'

Simon was suspicious. I was going to send him flying off when I had merely tried to bait a hook for him. I saw the cockchafer's wings stir again. I went on, very fast: 'Because of the true incident that helped to make me what you call an angel. One day at this Bordeaux fair I went into the "Dupuytren Museum". It showed wax models of anatomical specimens. The intention was ostensibly instructive, but there was also a representation of childbirth.'

'Had Madame given you permission?'

'No, I had gone by myself, for once in a while, with a friend. And then suddenly I saw . . . I shall always see it, yes, till my dying day . . . The label said: "Penis of a Negro, ravaged by syphilis."'

We stood for a few moments without saying a word. Simon suddenly asked me:

'Purity, now; what does that mean to you? What would you tell a seminarist who asked you why one must be pure?'

'So as to be able to give oneself. That was the answer I had from a young priest to whom I once happened to confess. The gift of one-self to others, he told me, which is our vocation, requires absolute purity. Then you can boldly venture into deep waters.'

'No, but see here, Monsieur Alain! Are you having me on? A moment ago you were promising me worldly success, and now you're talking about giving oneself, of being pure so as to be able to give oneself . . .'

He was sneering, proud of confronting me with my own inconsistencies. I took his hand. It was damp. I could feel that boneless sixth finger; it was like a little creature that would give out juice if you crushed it, as Laurent used to say when he was small. Overcoming my repulsion, I said:

'You don't understand me. True, on the plane of the argument with M. Duport, I cannot promise you anything other than a worldly success which, at its highest point, might make a prince of

you . . . a great prince, both in the eyes of the world and in God's;
for you might be called to fulfil the duties of a bishop, a cardinal
towards the faithful and towards the whole Church; but mind, at
every turn, all along that race for honours, at every turn of that
triumphal progress, you could leave it, renounce everything, become
a saint – and I know you aspire to be that, too.'

How did I know, except that foreknowledge was part of my role?

'Me a saint? Oh, bugger it!'

'Yes, a saint. Perhaps you won't be able to stand that race for
honours, you'll submerge yourself in some out-of-the-way parish,
or perhaps a novitiate. I can picture you, rather, as parish priest
among the poor, thrown to them like a piece of bread to the fish in a
tank.'

'And why shouldn't that be possible in Paris, among laymen,
where I'm going to be tried out?'

I held on to his hand, although by now it was soaking wet.

'No, Simon, if you go into that set, abandon all hope, the water
will close again over your head. I don't say you won't find certain
advantages there, but no possibility of escaping towards God.'

He bridled: 'What d'you know about it? God wouldn't ask your
leave. We are paid to know that His ways are not our ways; we've
had that dinned into us often enough.'

'I just know, that's all,' I said. 'You're not obliged to believe me;
but if you choose Paris, you're done for.'

I knew he had chosen. I knew it would all end badly for him. He
drew back his hand, I wiped mine on my handkerchief. He said in a
low voice: 'I'm leaving tomorrow morning before dawn.' Prudent
would drive him in the trap to Villandraut, where he would take the
train; nobody here would see him go.

'If only you won't talk.'

'No, Simon, I won't talk.'

A flock of sheep passed along the road, I heard the shepherd call out to them. Simon coughed. I repeated Mother's ritual phrase: 'You feel the coolness of the stream.' Simon insisted: I would say nothing? He admitted that there would be some advantage in my warning the Doyen and Mother so that they would feel the shock less, but without telling them it was so close. He went away along a path. I went back to the house just as Laurent was coming out, and he told me he was going to cut and run – the curé was there, and old Mother Duport into the bargain. Madame Duport? Laurent was not surprised, nothing surprised him.

The hanging lamp was alight in the hall, although it was not yet dark. The first thing I saw, sitting petrified in front of the Doyen and Mother, was Mme Duport in her crêpe veil, yellow-eyed, with something wild and dishevelled about her in spite of the care she must have taken with her appearance before coming to our house: a woman who drinks always gives herself away by something. As for Mother's expression, as she looked at this drink-sodden creature who perhaps had a fondness, a fancy for Simon! It's unbelievable, she must have been thinking, what goes on in other people. It was unbelievable that Mme Duport should be there, in our house.

'You know my son Alain?'

Mme Duport stared at me, her face a lifeless mask in spite of the birdlike or cowlike eye that suggested the product of some mythological mating. She answered, never taking her eyes off me, that Simon had often spoken of me to her. The Doyen then said that she could speak freely in my presence, that I must be told of the situation. But Mme Duport no longer wished to talk. She kept her solemn bovine gaze fixed on me. She belonged to the species that, I know, would like to eat me up.

It was M. le Doyen who told me the gist of Mme Duport's story: Simon was to study for his *licence* in Paris, doing it in a year if possible, and then he was to have a place in the secretariat of the Radical Party, in the Rue de Valois; but behind this façade a plot was

being hatched which Mme Duport had discovered, and which consisted in the detailed exploitation of Simon's recollections of
seminary life, both at school and at college. There was a great deal to
be got out of them, according to M. Duport. He had borrowed
Simon's notebooks, and was carefully going through the History
and Philosophy textbooks.

'How could Simon consent to it?'

'He was told that since he had been top of his class, it would greatly
improve his chances of an appointment if the judges were to see his
work.'

Mme Duport broke in then: 'Simon was far too clever not to
realize his treachery.'

I protested: 'Simon cannot have believed that his school notebooks would be of the least importance.'

In fact, what could anyone get out of them? His textbooks were a
different matter. Those in use at my own school, specially prepared
for Catholic pupils, were stuffed with absurdities of which Donzac
and I had drawn up a list. In any case, there could be nothing
treacherous about communicating what was already within everyone's reach. Simon had wanted to taste forbidden fruit. The Doyen
asked me if he had told me so.

'So I understood: the die is cast.'

The Doyen protested: 'No, he'll come back to us!' I shook my
head. I murmured: 'He's lost.'

'Lost for us, perhaps,' the Doyen said fervently, 'but not lost, no,
the poor child, not lost!'

I loved the poor priest at that moment. I assured him that I felt as
he did. As for Mother, she would keep silence as long as Mme
Duport was there; but Mme Duport seemed to have become part of
the armchair which she filled with her massive form. She was looking at me, not furtively; I could feel her eyes on me. Then Mother,
who knows on every occasion what's done and what is not done,

rose and obliged us all to rise, except Mme Duport, who must have sensed the dismissal implicit in my mother's gesture, softened by a formal phrase of thanks for the information she had brought us. Mme Duport got up at last, came towards me and said: 'You must come and see me before school starts. We'll talk about him.'

I excused myself, saying that term began in a fortnight.

'Surely not for you this year: you've passed your *bachot*. Simon told me you'd be staying at Maltaverne for the pigeon-shooting.'

So they talked about me together! These were the sort of people who were interested in me. Mlle Martineau never talked about me to anyone.

'Oh, I don't care for shooting . . .'

'Then you'll have all the more time.'

She wore the hermetic smile of people who want to hide their teeth. The curé, deeply shocked, said in an authoritative tone: 'I'll see you home, Madame,' and dragged her off to the front steps. As I was going down behind Mme Duport and the priest, Mother ordered me: 'No, stay!' We went back into the drawing-room. She dropped into an armchair and hid her head in her hands; in prayer, or in rage? I think she was trying to pray and fighting against the rage that broke out at last.

Poor Mother, everything I was dreading to hear her say came pouring forth. She reckoned up all she had spent on Simon for the past ten years. 'The more you do for them, the more they rob you. Oh, we've been properly swindled! . . . No, I'm exaggerating, I wasn't swindled since I had no illusions about him. As M. le Doyen says, you've got to give yourself, over and over again, knowing you'll get nothing in exchange.'

'That may be true for M. le Doyen, but not for us. Don't worry, you'll have got it all back from the old donkey.'

Mother asked me, disconcerted: 'What old donkey?'

'That old beast of burden of yours, Duberc, who looks after your

ten farms, for three hundred francs a year, and is the only person
who knows the boundaries of your lands, so that if he left us today
we should be at the mercy of all our neighbours . . .'

'Whose fault is it if you and your brother are a useless pair, if
you're not capable of knowing the boundaries . . .'

'You know these things can't be learnt, you have to belong to the
region and have lived there all your life. You've often seen Duberc
beating the bushes and digging the ground at some spot where
there's nothing outstanding, and then suddenly the boundary mark
appears among the brambles. You couldn't get along without him.
If he were to blackmail you and demand three times what you give
him it would still be incredibly little.'

'No, that's too bad! He has his house, with free heating and light-
ing, and he has milk and his share of the pig.'

'Yes, he wouldn't know what to do with the money you don't
give him. So he gives you his work for nothing.'

She moaned: 'You always take their side against me . . .'

At that moment the priest reappeared. He had taken Mme Duport
home and then pretended to go on to the presbytery.

'Now I'm back we must have a talk.'

'Certainly not in front of this little fool, who was so sure he could
make Simon change his mind and who now stands up for him and
blames me.'

'I'd promised nothing. I thought I knew what to say to Simon. I
wasn't mistaken, but it was too late.'

'In any case, you and I have done all we could,' Mother said to the
curé; she needed his approval, his sanction. He stood silent, looking
like Simon with his stalwart peasant build and his leanness – there
seemed no flesh on his great frame – and the face which he was
perpetually kneading looked like clay, with eyes like two glazed
drops. He stood silent, and she kept on at him: 'Yes or no, hadn't
they done all they could?' The curé's mumbled reply was a word in

our local *patois* which I don't know how to spell: *Beleou*, with the final *ou* barely stressed, and which means 'maybe'. No peasant would understand its meaning if he lived outside a twenty-mile radius round Maltaverne.

'We tried to give a priest to the Church.'

'That's putting it wrongly,' the curé said. 'We cannot dispose of another man's life, even to give it to God, and especially if he is materially dependent on us. What lay in our power to do, and what I thought I was trying to do for Simon, was to discover God's intentions towards this child, and to help him see clear within himself.'

I was struck by the curé's words: 'What I thought I was trying to do.' I could not contain myself and I muttered: 'Yes, but then you had other motives!' Mother had another 'hot flush': 'Apologize at once to M. le Doyen!'

The curé shook his head: why apologize? I had not offended him.

I looked at him. I hesitated, then at last I said to him: 'M. le Doyen, you seem to be as busily involved as the rest of us in this pitiful farce, but you spend your nights alone in a sordid presbytery with peeling walls, and in the morning you officiate at the altar in an almost empty church. You know all about it.'

'What's that to do with Simon?' Mother asked.

'It means that you're endlessly, monotonously defeated not so much by your adversaries as by your own supposed flock. Your enemies, at all events, prove by their hatred that the Church is still capable of arousing some sort of passion.'

The curé interrupted me: 'I had better go, you'll begin talking nonsense, as Madame says.'

He rose. Laurent came in just then. I hate the way he smells at the end of a summer's day, but I was glad he was there. By his mere presence he created an atmosphere in which tensions dissolved. Nothing seemed of any greater importance than the snares he had

just set, or Diane's pup which he was training with the aid of a
spiked collar, like the brute he was. Only the common herd believe
there's something important in the world – a comment of Barrès's
which Donzac is fond of repeating. I said:
    'I'll go with you to the church door, M. le Doyen.'
    The mist from the stream had not yet reached the avenue. The
curé said: 'There's a smell of autumn.' I muttered, whether in pity
or in spite I couldn't say: 'All that long winter ahead of you . . .' He
did not react. After a spell of silence he asked if I knew when Simon
was leaving.
    'I'm not asking you to tell me when. But you do know?'
    I said nothing. He did not persist, but as we drew near the church
door I asked him whether he still celebrated Mass at seven in the
morning.
    'May I come and serve for you tomorrow?'
    He understood, and grasped my hand; he would expect me.
    'I'll come a little earlier, to confess. Perhaps Mother will be there?'
    'No, it's not her day.' He made this reply rather hurriedly, as
though to reassure me and himself. He did not speak again until we
reached the presbytery. There he said, under his breath: 'I've been
wrong.' As I protested: 'No, no, M. le Doyen!' he insisted: 'I must
have been wrong about everything.'
    'Except the essential thing, M. le Doyen.'
    'What d'you mean?'
    'You believe in what you're doing. Perhaps you've been pouring
new wine into old bottles, those they handed down to you at the
seminary. But this new wine, you renew it every day, in spite of the
old bottles, of an out-of-date theology that's falling to pieces.'
    The curé sighed, and pulled my ear gently, muttering: 'You little
modernist!' and then said, tenderly: 'Come tomorrow.'

III

My memories of that early morning Mass, and of the scene between Duberc and Mother when she discovered that Prudent had driven Simon to Villandraut to catch the train have been overlaid by what happened at Maltaverne a few days later. But where shall I begin? I remember walking along the Jouanhaut road one of those evenings. I think the moon was rising; at all events, there was moonlight in my memory of it. The silence was such that as I crossed over the river I could hear the Hure running over the old stones. And everywhere, at that time of night, if I was to believe the books I loved, living creatures came together. Since the stage was set, the play must exist. Why not for me? Because only the setting is provided for us, and we have to provide all the rest ourselves; and I hadn't the strength, at eighteen . . . The strength for what? Neither for death nor for life. The toad I could hear croaking made me think of what my grandmother said a few days before her death (and yet she was a saintly woman), that she would sooner be a toad under a stone than die. As though to be a toad under a stone were not happiness, as though there were any other happiness in this world than to call one's mate gently and come together with her under the stones or in the tangled grass! It seems to me today that I had a presentiment that something was going to happen that night. The chilly breath from the stream against my face was that of death . . . But I may be inventing.

Mother was wandering along the garden walk, wrapped in a

shawl. She was probably saying her rosary. She warned me that Laurent was feeling ill and had gone to bed, and that I must be careful to make no noise.

'When I think that you make us share a room, as if we were short of rooms in this barracks of a house! I wonder what you can be thinking of.'

She did not take offence. She apologized. 'You've always been together.'

'That was because you insisted on it, whereas we've not got a single taste in common, Laurent and I, and we've never had anything to say to one another.'

Mother repeated her familiar reproach: 'You think everybody's stupid.'

'There's one idiot at any rate,' she went on in sudden fury, 'and that's Simon. When I think of all he's thrown overboard . . .'

'No, he's thrown away nothing that really matters. He'll keep what he has learnt, his bachelor's diploma – all that he owes to you, and that others will reap the benefit of, if that's any comfort to you.'

'That's not the point, you know perfectly well!'

'Anyhow that's the thing you cannot bear to think about. As for Simon's destiny, you cannot be specially concerned about that, since you don't love him. You're not going to tell me you love Simon? And even if you did love him, really love him, as Mme Duport loves him . . .'

'Go off to bed!'

'In that case you'd not be worrying about Simon's eternal destiny, since what you'd love would be the perishable part of him . . .'

She pushed me towards the stairs: 'Go up, keep quiet so as not to wake your brother and let me hear no more of you . . . This boy will be the death of me.'

I protested that it was too early to sleep. I was going to take a walk round the park.

'Put on something warm. One invalid's enough. And when you go to bed, don't open the window. Laurent has a cough.'

'He often coughs at night,' I said. 'He coughs in his sleep.'

'How do you know? You never wake up in the night.'

'I hear him in a half-sleep.'

I am certain I am not inventing this: I remember being upset myself by what I was saying, and feeling suddenly afraid for Laurent, as though as a result of wanting to upset other people I had fallen victim to my own evil spell, but the anguish lasted only a few seconds. And then I was myself again, in the milky darkness of a moonlight night, just as I always am at such times, aware of the purling sound of the Hure, of the calm whispering night, like any other night, of the same light that will shine on the stone under which the body that was myself will lie rotting. Time flows by like the Hure and the Hure is still there and will still be there and will still be flowing . . . It's enough to make one scream with horror. How can other people bear it? They seem not to know.

And meanwhile I didn't know that the night which was beginning with all its countless agonies . . . But I must tell these things without inventing them, and make an exact, factual report of them for Donzac. I went indoors. It was the year before Mother had electricity put in. A single lamp was burning over the billiard table. I took one of the candlesticks and went up to our room, which was over Mother's room. 'The boys' room', a big room with two windows, and our two beds were back to back so that Laurent and I could spend the whole night together without even seeing one another, and he almost always got up at dawn. In the evening, when we were small, he would drop off to sleep at the supper-table, and have to be carried up to bed. For the past two years he had taken to 'gadding about', as they said, and I'd be asleep when he crept in

furtively, carrying his shoes; when I woke in the mornings Laurent
had vanished long ago.

I was quite determined to open the window in spite of Mother's
orders. The air was close. I did not recognize Laurent's familiar
odour, a wholesome doggy smell. Fever has its own smell, and I was
immediately conscious of it. He was asleep, not snoring but breathing noisily. I had begun to undress when Mother came in, in her
dressing-gown, with her hair in a plait, and whispered to me that I
would find it difficult to sleep, that Laurent might need her, that
she would take my bed and I move into hers. I needed no pressing,
and without another glance at my brother I ran down to Mother's room
on the first floor. It was smaller than ours, because a *cabinet de toilette*
and a wardrobe had been fixed up in two corners, thus forming an
alcove in which the bed stood. I opened one of the windows with
relief and slipped into the bed in which I had been conceived. This
strange thought, fascinating and yet intolerable, I drove from me
with that instinctive reaction that I had retained from my scrupulous
childhood, convinced that one's eternal life may depend upon a
single thought.

To conquer the obsession, I had recourse to the device I often used
to glide gently into sleep. I told myself a story: I always had one on
the stocks. The current one delighted me particularly. I had read
that year for the first time Balzac's *Splendeurs et misères des Courtisanes*,
and, shocked by Lucien de Rubempré's suicide in prison, I had invented another version of the story: Lucien was not compromised or
imprisoned, Carlos Herrera succeeded in swindling Baron de
Nucingen of the huge sum needed to enable Lucien to marry the
daughter of the Duc de Grandlieu. I forestalled all difficulties.
Thanks to the support of the Duke and of Carlos Herrera, Lucien
became an attaché at the Embassy in Rome, so that the marriage was
performed almost secretly in the Embassy chapel, without anyone in

Paris knowing about it, thus averting any possible danger to Lucien. Soon after, Carlos Herrera decided to die and to be reincarnated in Jacques Collin, the escaped convict whom he really was. He pretended to have an incurable tumour; he went to be operated upon in a private hospital in Switzerland which was run by his gang. The corpse of another patient became Carlos Herrera's, and Jacques Collin made his escape . . . And then I slipped and sank into a deep, heavy sleep, from which I should emerge when the first sunbeam pierced through the shutters.

But that night I awoke in pitch darkness, feeling lost in a bed which was not mine and in which my mother's smell lingered. I knew at once that something was happening, I knew at once that it was something serious. Hurried footsteps echoed noisily along the passage, doors slammed. The thing was happening overhead. Laurent? The clatter of jugs and basins reassured me, he must have been sick. I turned over towards the wall. At that moment Mother came in, carrying a lamp that shone full on her long face and her dishevelled grey hair. She stood in the doorway: 'Listen, you'd better know . . . ' Laurent had been spitting blood; it was still going on. Dr Dulac and the Doyen were with him. I made as though to get up, but she begged me not to stir before dawn.

'Then you'd better go to the farm at Jouanhaut. You must get away, away,' she repeated wildly. 'I shan't breathe freely till I know you're far off.'

'But Laurent . . .'

'It's not a question of Laurent now, but of yourself.'

'But Maman, Laurent? Laurent?'

She stood as though turned to stone, her lamp in her hand and a long lock of white hair streaking her forehead. Her burning gaze was fixed on me.

'Pray for your poor brother, but our first duty is to isolate you. God grant it's not too late. When I think you've been sharing his room in Bordeaux and at Maltaverne for years now. And only last night you were breathing the same air as him.'

'But what about Laurent, Maman . . .'

'We'll do our utmost, you can be sure. We're having a specialist in tomorrow. But you've got to know . . .' She hesitated. 'The doctor thinks . . .' She broke off, and reverted to a detailed account of her plans for me. It seemed as if I alone were involved in this disaster, as though it were important and momentous only in relation to myself. I was to go without clothes or linen except what I had with me, all my things being in the contaminated room.

'I shan't even kiss you, and of course you won't go near Laurent's room. In any case he's not fit . . . It's better you shouldn't remember him so . . .'

'Not the last time, Maman, not the last time!'

'Why, you know I always imagine the worst. I'm going to fetch you some coffee. Go back to bed.'

I would let her have her way, I would do what she wanted. She had frightened the youth of nineteen as she used to frighten the small boy, to get him to obey. At Maltaverne there had been the room and the bed where Grandfather had died, and at Bordeaux the room and the bed where Father had died. And here there would be the room and the bed where Laurent . . . Suddenly he ceased to be an insignificant dunce and began to exist in a new form within my mind. He had never said a single word that was not about pigeons, snipe, or hares, or hounds. He was studying for Grignon, but he was as indifferent to agricultural book-learning as to Latin or Hebrew. He had always said: 'I shall be the peasant of the family', but he looked after nothing at Maltaverne.

'You leave me to do everything,' Mother used to lament, although she would never have allowed us to meddle in the slightest way with

her affairs, which in fact were our own since Maltaverne belonged
to us and she was merely our guardian.

My thoughts were wandering thus and suddenly stumbled up
against this: 'Now there will only be me, I shall be alone at Maltaverne, face to face with Mother.' Yes, that thought came into my
mind, but as God's my witness it gave me no satisfaction, since it was
impossible that Mother should not have thought of it too, with her
maniacal passion for the land, and that she should not have been
obscurely affected by it. She adored the land, but not as I did; she
hated anything being shared out . . . Donzac, for whom I am writing
this, doesn't need to be told: nothing of all this was clear in my mind
during that ghastly night, nothing was admitted, accepted, recognized. I am setting out the thoughts that came into my mind during
those hours that have marked me so indelibly in the order and
sequence that I gave them later, during the week that followed,
while I was staying with the maiden ladies at Jouanhaut.

I waited for daybreak lying fully dressed on mother's bed. She
came back once without crossing the threshold of the room, to
bring me some coffee and tell me that Marie Duberc was busy iron-
ing my linen and that I would have all I needed. I only had to collect
my books and my scribbles, as she called everything that I wrote. I
dozed off. I was vaguely conscious of hearing the wheels of Duberc's
cart. Marie came in with a tray, her head tied up in the black scarf
old women wear; she was all in black herself, like a shiny black hen
with her startled eyes and round rump. Since Simon's flight, at
which they had connived, Mother no longer spoke to the Dubercs
except to give them orders. Marie assured me that Laurent was
resting now, that Madame was by his side. The doctor was sending
for a Sister of Mercy from the hospital at Bazas. Marie moaned:
'Ah! Lou praou moussu Laurent!' He was the Dubercs' favourite:
'Ah! Lou praou!'

I shall never forgive myself for having run away without a last sight of my dying brother. Mother kept guard to prevent me from entering the room; through the half-open door I caught a brief glimpse of displaced furniture and scattered linen, seen by the tremulous glimmer of a night-light. I put up no resistance; everything took place as Mother had decided. At nineteen, I let her manage me as if I were a newborn child. I protested feebly, she did not even listen. She said: 'As soon as the crisis is over, you shall see him again. I promise you that. I'll send for you. You shall talk to him from a distance, there'll still be some fine weather to come, and we'll have him sitting in the park, in the sun. The forest air will do him more good than anything.'

Ah, the mist of that September morning, the smell of it . . . But I am not going to die; I am going to live. Mother had sent a message to the Jouanhaut ladies, warning them of my arrival and of our misfortune. Mlle Louise and Mlle Adila were waiting for me, their delight at my unexpected arrival confusedly mingled with compassion and grief. But joy predominated, particularly in the case of Mlle Adila, condemned by fate to live with a deaf woman who understood everything by lip-reading, seven miles away from the village, in that remote region where the only road petered out while beyond the great empty *lande* stretched out as far as the sea. It was one of those old-fashioned farms at the edge of a vast field of millet, from one of which, so I like to think, we originally came. That morning the larks were singing above the field, but Laurent would never shoot larks again. An enormous musty-smelling room, facing the sunrise, had been got ready for me; I knew that the ladies' father had committed suicide there after his ruin, but they did not know that I knew. I laid on the table the Brunschvicg *Pascal*, a typed copy of *Action* by Maurice Blondel, lent me by Donzac, and Bergson's *Matière et Mémoire*; and I went at once to forage in the bookcase of the 'parlour', which when I was a child had yielded me a joy so intense that it seems to me that those who have not felt it know nothing of the miracle that reading can be, when no breath from outside disturbs the smooth surface of a day in the summer holidays, when the real landscape chimes with one's dream landscape and when the very smell of the house dwells within one, just as it will dwell unchanged long after the house itself has ceased to exist.

What I was reading was not Bergson nor Pascal nor the *Annales de Philosophie chrétienne*, but *Les Enfants du capitaine Grant, L'Ile mysterieuse, Sans famille*. And yet Laurent's bedroom, as I had glimpsed it through the half-open door in the tragic gleam of the nightlight, lingered within me. I never ceased to be aware of it, I fed my grief and anguish on it, yet perhaps, too, my happiness at being nineteen and overflowing with life.

I heard Mlle Adila, who had formed the habit of shouting to her sister, telling the cook: 'If the worst should happen, what a fine match M. Alain will be, with his three thousand hectares . . .'

'Why yes, to be sure, but so long as his mother's alive she'll be the mistress . . .'

'Shut up, you silly woman,' shouted Mlle Adila. 'His mother has her own estate, nearly a thousand hectares of land and a house fully furnished at Roaillon, and plenty of ready money, Heaven knows!'

'Yes, but . . .'

I went out so as to hear no more. Laurent was still living, he was alive; Mother loved us both. The Doyen came that afternoon to bring me news: 'Your mother is wonderful, as usual. She sits up with Laurent part of the night so that the Sister of Mercy can sleep. She's determined not to see you even from a distance. She's consented to make that sacrifice. Alas, there's not much longer to wait.' For the first time that day I heard the fatal words: 'galloping consumption.' That gallop seemed to reverberate in my own mind, carrying my elder brother away for ever into a darkness where I would myself follow him, at a slower pace if not at a gallop; and however slowly I moved on I should end up like the old man of Lassus, with my three thousand hectares and a horde of heirs who would pester me, whom I should hate and, like him, keep at a distance. I felt a horror of property; possession seemed an absolute evil. How could I be free of it? I would gladly renounce this world's goods, but not the world itself, not that wild excessive joy that had overwhelmed me that day, under the oak trees at Jouanhaut, while my brother was being carried off at the gallop into the night that will have no end.

The microbe of the property-disease appeared next morning, as though falling out of the sky, visible to the naked eye, in the shape of a horrible little girl of ten, Jeannette Séris, the ladies' heir, who came in that capacity to visit them and be worshipped by the farm people. The curious thing was that, being an only child, this little horror would some day own one of the vastest estates in the *lande*, which would swallow up the ladies' property like a drop of water. But for these land-hungry creatures every hectare counted. Jeannette repelled me: a pale freckled child, who looked as if two of her freckles had turned phosphorescent and taken the place of eyes, without brows or lashes. Her scanty hair was pulled back from her forehead with a round comb. The tenants' children were sent for to play with her. '*Que diz a mamizelle?*' They were as submissive to her as little muzhiks to little boyars in the days of serfdom. Next morning when I woke up I heard Mlle Louise shouting to Mlle Adila: 'But he's barely ten years older than she is. He can wait!' Mlle Adila must have answered simply by moving her lips, for I heard no more. The deaf woman persisted: 'He won't marry without his mother's leave. He'll wait as long as is necessary . . . ' Oh God! They were talking about me and Jeannette. The match had been discussed in the neighbourhood, much as in old days people had discussed the betrothal of the Dauphin to the Spanish Infanta. But this time I was the only nominee; Laurent no longer shared the appalling risk. The thing must have already been settled in Mother's mind, I was convinced of that. To crown it all, the horrible child pursued me, with her airs and graces; she had the same thing in mind. It was during that week that I became ashamed of my ignorance and indifference about all social questions. I resolved to read Jaurès, Guesde, Proudhon, Marx . . . These were only names to me. In any case I knew better than they did what property was. If it were merely robbery I shouldn't care, but it is something that debases and degrades mankind.

IV

Now, two years later, at Bordeaux, I am starting a fresh notebook. As for the first, Donzac begged me to let him take it with him to Paris, where he has entered the Carmelite Seminary. It is for his sake that I have decided to take up this journal once more. Hardly a journal: an account of the day-to-day experiences in Mother's and my story, to which I have tried to give some shape and order; and above all an attempt to see clearly what I have myself become since the death of Laurent.

What I have become? Am I different from what I was? Is the young man of twenty-one, studying for his *licence de lettres* at Bordeaux, a different person from the adolescent I once was? No, the same, and doomed to remain the same unless, like Laurent, I die. The old man of Maltaverne who dwells within me will succeed to the old man of Lassus in the secret history of our province, our great *lande*, and at eighty will still be the same person that I am now, while some child-poet in 1970 will watch him from a distance, as he sits motionless, in his doorway, turned to stone.

What Laurent's death has altered is not myself but the conditions of my life. For months I was stunned. Mother took charge of everything; she was solely concerned about my physical health. I had 'a faint patch on my left lung'. She did not rest until she had secured my exemption from military service. I was pleased, yet I could have died of shame. It made me more unsociable than ever and I held it against her. Now that she is relieved of this worry she spends more and more time at Maltaverne; since we bought a car this year, a Dion-Bouton, she goes there constantly for brief visits. Distance has been abolished. Only last year we had to change trains twice to reach Maltaverne. From the moment you entered the Gare du Midi at Bordeaux, you felt you were on a long journey, and the great *lande*, my only beloved home, was as remote as a star. Today I know that the *lande* begins at the very gates of Bordeaux and that, provided the carburettor does not let us down and no tyres burst, we can cover the hundred kilometres between Bordeaux and Maltaverne in under three hours.

I am writing whatever comes into my head so as not to touch that painful spot that has festered ever since Laurent fell asleep. What has happened between Mother and myself? What can I blame her for? She has taken charge of everything, she has released me from all cares. When she is at Maltaverne, as is the case just now, I am as free at Bordeaux as any student can ever have been, with a cook and a manservant to attend to my needs. If I'm incapable of taking advantage of this, it is surely not Mother who should be blamed for it.

'Why haven't you any friends? Why do you refuse all invitations, or stand about in corners not dancing?'

I don't dance, just as I don't shoot. It's just the same . . .

No, nothing is just the same. What I am going to tell is past history and not history in the making, although it is still going on. Donzac will know how to distinguish between the document thus interpreted and touched up by myself and the story that is taking shape from day to day and from page to page and is part of an ineluctable fate. Donzac will be able to interpret my lies by omission, and make them tell the truth without my knowing it – that truth which, nevertheless, I should like to extract from myself by force, which I seek with a passion that frightens me, not on my own account but because Mother is involved, because I am gradually unmasking her and the more I discover of her true features, the more they terrify me.

But I'm not alone now. I am no longer in her hands. Someone has come. Someone. It all began in Bard's bookshop in the Galleries that run between the Rue Sainte-Catherine and the Place de la Comédie. It was some time before I discovered this dark cavern full of books. My own particular bookshop was Féret's in the Cours de l'Intend- ance. At Bard's the *Mercure de France* editions have the place of honour; literature is cherished there, and the windows are full of modern poetry.

I have been there almost daily on my way back from the Faculty, ever since that first day when I had begun to glance through the pages of a new book, *L'Immoraliste*, so deeply fascinated by what I was reading that I started when I heard a woman's voice in my ear: 'Even if you haven't much money I advise you to buy it. It's a first edition, and first editions of Gide . . .'

I looked up and saw, amidst the gloom, Mlle Marie who is in charge of sales and who runs the whole shop (Bard, the owner, never leaves the cash desk and Balège, the hunchback assistant, does the chores). Mlle Marie, dressed in a black overall, makes herself invisible except to those on whom her eyes dwell as, that first day, they dwelt on me. There was tenderness mingled with mockery in that gaze, and a terrifying perspicacity. She was attracted and touched, as are all those who love me, by something in me that repels those who do not. And yet I deceived her without meaning to. I love books so much and I buy so few, and I hesitate for so long before making up my mind, and in a word I am so incapable of spending a single franc, and dress so badly into the bargain, always wearing the same stringy tie, that she mistook me for a poor student. I learned later that she had none the less been struck by the fact that my coat, shabby though it seemed, was not a ready-made garment, and that my briefcase was of good leather and bore my initials. But I seemed to have no pocket-money to spend. She thought I must be the son of a ruined or miserly country family, and she set aside first editions for me. 'You can pay next month,' she would tell me.

It was no base feeling that kept me from undeceiving her. A sort of shame? No, rather the joy of being loved for my own sake, of knowing that I could attract a girl of her quality, who did not know that I was the heir to Maltaverne. At those rare parties to which Mother makes me go to watch others dancing, I know that all the girls look at me in the same way; an invisible label is fastened to my dinner jacket: thousands of acres, country estates. They all smile the same meek smile, make the same efforts to talk about 'what sounds interesting'. These ninnies' conception of an 'intellectual' . . . No, I don't want to think about it. I only want Donzac to understand that unhoped-for happiness from the day it started, the love in that girl's eyes for the poor student that she thought I was. I learned later that she attributed my reluctance to go out with her to a fear of compromising her, so angelic did I seem to her, and since then we have laughed at it together. But I did not tell her the real reason, and indeed I am not sure of knowing it myself. It was partly the impossibility of keeping up for any length of time the legend of the poor student, once we were outside the shadowy cave of the bookshop; it was chiefly that I could no more think of her apart from the bookshop, with which I associated her, than I had thought of Mlle Martineau except on horseback. This was what protected me from her, while allowing me to get pleasure from her, as though there had been no other pleasure conceivable for me than to gaze at her in the enchanted semi-darkness of the bookshop, undisturbed by any sordid external problem, which I should have been quite incapable of solving.

.   .   .   .   .

This situation might have lasted indefinitely because Marie had come to accept it herself, because it corresponded to the image she had of me in her heart, what she called my *noli me tangere* side. But for a chance encounter . . . But I do not believe in chance, and coincidences may perhaps prove that our lives are really planned for us.

Although she was the moving spirit of the bookshop, her employer and his assistant did not approve of the way she allowed too many customers, of whom I was the most constant, to come and handle books which they did not buy. Her concept of a bookshop was that of Anatole France, who in *L'Orme du Mail* describes M. Bergeret meeting his friends every day in Paillot's bookshop. She confided to me that she often had to put up a fight on my behalf, and also on that of a young master at the little Lycée at Talence, who spent every Thursday afternoon – it was his one free day – in the bookshop. This was the day when I stayed away myself because the shop was crowded on a Thursday. 'He's as unsociable as yourself, he knows nobody.' 'But he knows you!' I said resentfully.

This resentment made her smile; she assumed that I was jealous. Was I really? In any case I looked so hurt that I promptly became jealous, believing that one learns to love (as, according to Pascal, one acquires piety) by 'bending the machine'.

I inquired anxiously as to the age of my unknown rival. He was several years older than myself. She felt sorry for him because of his utter solitude and the hopeless bitterness which some of his remarks betrayed, as if from his earliest days he had suffered some irreparable disaster. She spoke of him with a sympathy that seemed to increase the more vexation I showed – a vexation which was not assumed, which I really felt, and which Marie presently found unbearable. We were by ourselves at the moment, behind the secondhand book counter. For the first time she took my hand and held it for a moment in her own.

'When I think,' she said, 'that I don't even know your first name.

I know your initial, I've seen it on your briefcase. Which names begin with A? You're surely not called Arthur or Adolphe, or Auguste?'

'Maybe Augustin.' I put my lips close to her little ear: 'Alain . . .' I whispered, as if it were a great secret, and she repeated Alain, as if she were afraid of forgetting. I asked her: 'What did you call me when you thought about me?'

'I didn't call you anything. On the days when you didn't come I used to say to myself "the angel hasn't been today".'

'Oh,' I sighed, 'you, too?'

And at that moment I recalled that twilight scene at Maltaverne when Simon had said to me: 'Oh, you, you're an angel.' I thought of him at the precise moment when he was about to reappear in my life; this seems to me so strange that I suspect myself of unconsciously arranging the story, putting it into shape. But in fact this was just how it all happened. I remember going to the doorway without saying goodbye, while Marie followed me asking, in a low tone: 'What's the matter? I didn't mean to hurt your feelings.'

'Girls don't like angelic boys,' I said. (We were standing close together in the doorway; there were no customers left in the shop.) 'And they're quite right.'

'Because there are some bad angels?' asked Marie, with a forced laugh, trying to dispel this cloud.

'No, they would love a bad angel, he would make them suffer . . .'

'That depends on the sort of girl,' she said. 'I've never been fond of brutes, you know. I've always been afraid of them.'

'Whereas with me you feel safe.'

'Whatever I say offends you.'

'Are you afraid of the little teacher from Talence who comes every Thursday?'

'Oh, if you're distressing yourself on his account! Poor fellow, I find it so hard, and I don't always manage, to hide from him the fact that he repels me. I force myself to take his hand and even hold it in mine for a few moments, and this is quite an effort. You won't believe it, but he has six fingers on each hand. What I feel when I touch that limp bit of gristle . . .'

I had leaned back against the shop window. I asked: 'Simon? Is he in Bordeaux?'

'You know him? How do you know him?'

'Did you know he has an extra toe on each foot too? Well, Marie, next Thursday, tell him that one of your customers is called Alain and that he's an angel, and then you'll learn all about me, about my mother, about my childhood, about my part of the world, which is also Simon Duberc's. I'm not going to speak of him today because I couldn't do so without pouring out the whole of my wretched life, and I haven't the strength for that. I'll let him clear the ground . . . I'll merely have to touch up his account. When he's told you part of it, I shan't find it so hard to involve you in a story which is devoid of interest for anyone.'

She whispered: 'Except for me.' Then she told me the little she herself knew about Simon. He had found Paris unbearable and as soon as he had passed his *licence* had sought from the powerful patrons of whom he boasted an appointment in the Bordeaux region.

'But he tells me he'd be even lonelier here than in Paris, but for me.'

'Doesn't he go to see his parents?'

She did not know. He never spoke of them, as if he were ashamed of them. It crossed my mind that if he had been to Maltaverne my mother would have been bound to hear of it. I said goodbye, and opened the door. Then suddenly I envisaged the evening that lay ahead of me, and I shuddered. Everything that had kept me from going out with Marie was suddenly swept away. She would soon know all about me and my people. I did not even ask her if she was

free, I told her: 'You mustn't leave me alone tonight. Mother is in
the country. She's deserted me. I'll tell you all about it.' I deliberately
tried to make Marie anxious; but her joy prevailed over her
anxiety. She told me to go with her as far as her home: 'I'll run up
for a moment, just to let my mother know and put on another
frock.' The shop would close in half an hour. We arranged to meet
in front of the Grand Théâtre.

It was my first date, and I was twenty-one! I was not going to
spend that evening by myself. I went into the Café de Bordeaux and
rang up Louis Larpe, our butler, to warn him I was bringing a
friend to dinner. I could picture his stupefaction: 'A lady, Monsieur
Alain?' 'Yes, a lady.' 'I believe there's only one tournedos for
Monsieur.' 'You must open a tin of pâté de foie gras and get a
bottle of wine ready, whatever you like.'

I waited in the fog, in front of the one-story-house in the Rue de
l'Eglise Saint-Seurin where Marie lived, while she changed her dress.
When she reappeared, she was herself and yet someone else; she had
escaped from her job, from the gloomy bookshop, and I, for the first
time, stepped out proudly, like any other young man, in that
November evening the smell of which I shall never forget as long as
I live, eager to reach the Place Gambetta and the Cours de l'Intendance, and – dare I admit it? – to be seen with this young woman.
This made me ask Marie: 'Does it embarrass you to be seen on the
Intendance with a young man? We could go round by the back
streets.' She laughed: 'Oh, you know, as far as I'm concerned . . . It's
you, rather, who might find me compromising . . .' I told her that
we were from the Bazas region and had few acquaintances in
Bordeaux. All the same I had to prepare her, during the ten minutes
we should take to reach the Rue de Cheverus, where I lived, for
the luxurious house, the manservant . . . 'We've two thousand

hectares of pine forest, you know!' I said stupidly. The figure did
not seem to impress her. Like a fool, I added: 'Not to mention all
the rest.'

'That's nothing to boast about.'

'I'm not boasting, but I hadn't told you. I've got to warn you
now . . .'

'No, Alain, this alters everything. I won't dine at your mother's
house in her absence, and without her knowledge. I'm going to take
you to a little restaurant I know in the harbour: Eyrondo's.'

I protested that this was impossible, that I had already rung up
home to order a dinner worthy of her.

'Well, you can ring up from Eyrondo's and counter-order it.'

'You don't know Louis Larpe, that's our butler. I should never
dare . . . He's opened a tin of foie gras. That's a religious ritual for
him. Besides I hate telephoning, I've done it for you, but I can't get
used to it. I scarcely ever telephone.'

'Aren't you ashamed?'

'Yes, I'm ashamed. Mother keeps telling me: you think yourself
intelligent, but you're a poor creature.'

'It was high time I came!'

'Are you disgusted with me?'

'No, because in spite of your thousands of acres you'll never fit in
to that society, you'll never be one of them . . . I see some of them in
my job, not many, for they're not much given to reading. But still I
have some customers who collect rare books. I watch them: a shop
counter is a fine barricade! I listen to them, I spy on them across it, I
know them.'

'But you don't know me, Marie. When you come to know
me . . .'

We were sitting at the back of the restaurant, which must once
have been a fishermen's tavern and where people now came to eat

shellfish, lampreys, and *cèpes* when they were in season. Marie had
gone to the counter to telephone my home. She had come back
laughing – I hadn't known she could laugh like that: 'Don't worry! I
heard the butler call out to the cook :"he's counter-ordered, just as
well I didn't open the tin of pâté." Now are you happy?'

'I'm ludicrous,' I said piteously.

When I recall that evening I am stupefied at the urgent need I felt
to unburden myself, the indiscretion with which I talked about myself inexhaustibly, as if this girl or young woman about whom I was
totally ignorant had had nothing to confide to me about her own
life, as if it went without saying that I was the only one of us two
who was interesting. She listened to me that evening without asking
me a single question other than those I needed to get relief from
what was choking me.

'Simon Duberc will tell you more about it than I dare.'

'But if you'd rather, I won't speak to him about you.'

I protested that on the contrary I wanted her to get a sombre
picture of Maltaverne from a man who had become our enemy.

'Besides, he won't speak ill of me, unless he has changed completely; he used to be fond of me.'

I asked, after a silence: 'Did he confess to you that he was educated in a seminary and had worn a soutane?'

'Ah! Now I understand why he gives the impression of being an
outsider . . . He has been moulded and remoulded by the priests and
then discarded . . .'

I hesitated before asking: 'Does religion mean anything to you,
Marie?'

'What about yourself, Alain? I'm asking you, but I know the
answer.'

How did she know? I repeated: 'What about you, Marie?' She
said 'It's of no interest,' and added: 'The die is cast as far as I'm

concerned, on all counts; I'm twenty-eight. I wanted to tell you my age, in case you might think me capable of day-dreaming about you.'

I asked: 'Why not?' and then rose hurriedly, as though seized with panic: 'Let's get out of here!'

'And the bill, Alain dear?'

When we were on the sidewalk of the embankment, which was already deserted save for a few suspicious-looking figures, I wanted to return as fast as possible to the Place de la Comédie. There have been a number of crimes committed in the streets after midnight. She told me, laughing, that I had drunk almost the whole of the bottle of Margaux by myself and that she did not really believe all I had told her about Maltaverne.

'You must believe me, Marie. As you'll find out, it's the sort of story nobody could have invented, and besides Simon will confirm it. Until my brother's death I had always believed, and so had everyone else, that I was my mother's favourite. My happiness lay in believing it. After Laurent was gone the shameful thought occurred to me, and indeed I dwelt on it complacently, that now there would only be myself and her, yes, I was actually capable of thinking that now nobody in the world could come between us. It was the exact reverse: before long I had to face the fact that never, at any moment in my life, had I felt so remote from her, that never had we been more cut off from one another. What stood between us was not a person. You won't believe me when I tell you it was the estates . . .'

'What estates?' Marie asked in a weary tone, and less from interest than from politeness.

'Ours, or rather mine, since Maltaverne comes to me from my father's side and since I had inherited Laurent's share. But Mother, who runs everything, and to whom I have handed over all my powers, considers herself absolute mistress of them. Of course I'd

been aware of her passion, not for the land in the way I love it, but
for property . . .'

'How dreadful!' said Marie.

'No, it's not so vile as you think. It's a love of power, the desire to
rule over a vast estate.'

'Over a people of serfs. You're still in the feudal era. Oh, take me
home! I daren't go back by myself . . .'

'But Marie, I'm on the side of the victims in all this. Yes, I'll take
you home, but just listen a little longer: until Laurent's death, and
while we were still children, Mother's passion was betrayed only on
rare occasions. She was our guardian. The estates were her responsibility. What changed everything, I believe, after my brother's
death, was the certainty that there would be no division of the
property, that her empire would remain intact.'

'It's monstrous.'

'More so than you could imagine. One of our neighbours at
Maltaverne, Numa Séris, who is a sort of cousin of ours, has the
largest estate in the region next to ours; he's a widower, whose wife
died of grief . . .'

'People don't die of grief,' Marie said irritably.

'How Numa Séris has survived the apéritifs, the tots of brandy,
the red wine that he consumes all day long, his sole source of happiness in life, is a mystery that has never much aroused my curiosity.
On the other hand, I was surprised to find my mother visiting him.
She pretended to be asking his advice about the sale of some timber,
or some disagreement with her tenant farmers; but I soon discovered the bond that lay between her and that contemptible
creature. He has a horrible daughter, whom Laurent and I detested;
her name's Jeannette, but we always called her the Louse. I remember Laurent saying to me shortly before he died: "I'm lucky to
be too old for the Louse. You're the one who will marry the Louse."
And now suddenly the horrible farce has become a direct threat . . .'

'Why a threat? You're not a young girl who can be forced into marriage; admit that there's a part of yourself that is your mother's accomplice and dreams of this abominable match, and that what you're frightened of is that accomplice-self.'

We had reached her door. She had her key in her hand. She said: 'Good-bye, Alain. Don't come to the bookshop till Friday. I shall have seen Simon Duberc the day before. Then perhaps I shall see things in a different light.' The door slammed. I stood there alone, on the pavement of that narrow street in the Saint-Seurin district. I crouched on the doorstep with my elbows on my knees and I wept. My despair was not feigned and yet, in the strict sense, it was; my grief was self-indulgent; and nevertheless real tears were flowing between my fingers and I was vainly choking down real sobs.

The door opened again behind me. I stood up. Marie appeared, holding a lamp; she had not taken off her hat. She said: 'Luckily I saw you through the peephole.' She made me come in, warning me to make as little noise as possible, although her mother's bedroom looked over the courtyard; she took me into a narrow room which must have been the parlour. It was cold there, and smelt unused. The few pieces of furniture were hidden under dust-sheets; even the chandelier was covered with glazed cloth. Marie drew me down beside her on the sofa. I went on weeping, and she said: 'What a child you are! You're not even a boy of fifteen, you're a ten-year-old! I feel like asking you: "what's the big trouble then?"'

She took me in her arms. I hid my face between her shoulder and her neck. She kept as still as if a bird had alighted on her finger, and I was astonished at such peace, such happiness. I was learning my first steps: I was allowing myself to be 'touched', literally. I had ceased, by my own consent, to be 'intact'. She dried my eyes with her hand-kerchief, then touched them briefly with her lips and more linger-ingly with her hand, which was cold. At one point she stroked my

cheek, lightly; nothing more. I began to talk again, and she to
listen patiently.

'I'm ashamed,' I said, 'to have given you that atrocious picture of
my poor mother. I can see that the story I told you is unbelievable.
How can I make you understand what my mother is like? The only
time I ventured to speak to her myself of her plans about the Séris
girl, and explain the reason for my aversion, she would discuss none
of them, because in all sincerity, and incredible as it may seem to you,
she has always been convinced that what I call physical love doesn't
exist for creatures of a certain race, to which she and I belong, that
it's a romantic fiction, that sex is a duty required of woman by God
for the propagation of the species and as a remedy for man's bestial
nature; she freely admitted that it's the most puzzling aspect of
creation for her. I agreed with her that the close association of a soul,
capable of knowing God, with an animal body, opened an abyss
before one's mind. She protested violently that this was an ordeal
which Christians had to overcome, in the first place, by not letting
themselves be seduced by the lies they read in books – which were
my whole life; "but you're my son," she added, "and I know you,
and I know you'll feel the same disgust for those things, for that
thing . . . You can't know . . ."

At that moment I thought of my father, that father whom I had
never known, the mildest and gentlest of men. I muttered: "Poor
Father . . ." She said resentfully, in a near-whisper: "Oh, I give you
my word he spared me nothing. I never flinched." I repeated: "Poor
Father." After a pause, I remember, I asked my mother if she would
feel no remorse at handing over the wretched Jeannette to a husband
like myself, who would certainly shun her. "But my dear child, so
much the better for her! when she's given you a son you'll leave her
in peace, and she will still have the glory of having helped to create
an estate which will be the finest in all the Bazadais in extent and in
the value of the land, and will give her, the little Séris girl, control

over the welfare of a dependent population: the only legitimate pleasure granted in this world to a woman from one of our families . . .'"

Poor Mother! When Marie expressed surprise that I had not brought home to her how shocking, in a professed Christian like herself, was this idolatrous worship of the land, I explained: 'Oh, she had plenty of arguments to justify her there, it's easy to invoke one's social responsibility. For Mother, evil consists in those covetous desires from which in fact she is immune, which she calls concupiscence and for which she feels only repulsion. She never thinks of sin in connection with her own pride in possession and domination. Has she ever read, I mean pondered over, certain of our Lord's words that I myself find terrifying? . . . No, that's not true; I'm no more terrified than she is.'

Then we were both silent.

A little later I whispered: 'What would Mother say if she saw us?'

'Aren't you cold?'

'No, you're as warm as a nest.'

Marie quoted softly: '*le premier'tu'qui sort des lèvres bien-aimées.*' I corrected her: '*le premier oui*' . . .'

A little later still, she drew back my hair from my forehead and put her lips there; and it was my turn to quote Verlaine:

' . . . *et qui parfois vous baise au front comme un enfant.*'

For a little while we kept still, making no other gesture. Suddenly she sat up and took my head between her two hands: 'Leave her! Yes, leave your mother, let her keep it all and go and live by yourself.'

I said sadly: 'Nothing can prevent its all belonging to me.'

'You're the property of your property. You'll marry the Louse.'

I clung closer to her. I said, after a silence: 'How can I leave Mother? She's been my whole life. The terrible thing, you see, isn't that she's taken possession of the lands that belong to me, but that she loves them better than me.'

'She's betrayed you with them!'

'That's so true that perhaps with your help I shall end by escaping from her.'

'What can I do for you, my poor dear? Make you more self-aware and thus unhappier, but not infuse into you a willpower that you haven't got!'

I protested that she had changed me, none the less, more than I could ever have imagined a few weeks ago, that now I realized that happiness might lie in escaping from my mother, but that I did not see how I could do without her, being incapable of looking after the estate myself. I was not ashamed to admit that it was dearer to me than anything else in the world. Maltaverne was my greatest love. On the other hand Numa Séris's lands meant nothing to me. And yet I was afraid of the Louse. All my life I had heard my mother boast that she had always attained her goal. When she wanted a stretch of pinewood she would wait for years, maybe, but she'd get it in the end. She was kept informed of the tiniest plot that was for sale, either by the lawyer or by Numa Séris. They kept up the game between them, each standing aside in turn. I happened to be the master card in their final scheme – the one to which, ever since Laurent's death, Mother had clung with a passion which she no longer disguised, but which sometimes broke forth so violently that it seemed utterly impossible for me ever to escape from it.

Marie asked me how old the Louse was and was relieved to hear she was only twelve. 'But my poor dear, you've at least seven or eight years in which to ward off the attack, and in the first place by getting married. The Louse wouldn't even be worth a single thought if you didn't belong both to your mother and to Maltaverne; they've each got a hold on you.'

'Yes, but now you're here.'

She moved away a little, and hummed: '*il faut nous séparer. C'est l'heure du sommeil*', and opened the street door to me.

I went striding down the middle of the empty street. The joy, the strength I felt within me were now turned against my mother. Hitherto my feelings had lagged behind the judgment I had passed on her. Now, this evening, everything coincided: I now experienced the same repulsion which Marie had involuntarily displayed, and in addition, as my footsteps clattered up our solemn old staircase, I felt an inordinate resentment at Mother's desertion of me, her crime in not loving me above everything else. But it was worse than that. Her love for me was infinitely less than the joy she felt in reigning, like an old Queen Regent, over her son's kingdom, while she was preparing to sacrifice that son, indeed had already sacrificed him in her mind, by marrying him to the Louse, with no excuse, without even the excuse of not knowing what physical love is. She had seen my father suffer. O my father, unknown but dearly loved; I remember once when I was ten or twelve, on my way back from school one evening, being suddenly struck, obsessed, by the thought that you were not dead. I don't remember what story I made up, that you had come back from a long voyage, that I should find you when I got home. I ran like a lunatic, jostling passers-by, I rushed, four steps at a time, up this same staircase. Under the Chinese lamp, Mother was hearing Laurent recite his catechism. Opposite her stood poor father's armchair, empty. Father, there was nothing left of you but your photograph, enlarged by Nadar, hanging over Mother's bed . . .

V

I was at the bookshop by five o'clock, and in spite of her frown I could see at a glance that Marie was glad I had disobeyed her; but her last customers were pestering her. She told me to come back for her in half an hour. It was raining; I walked about sheltering my pride and happiness under an umbrella. I studied my reflection in shop windows. Now I no longer looked like an angel, but like a boy with whom a girl was in love. And not just any girl. I was not blinded by love: she was far superior to her social rank (that bourgeois concept of rank, as if it were surprising that Marie should surpass the idiotic girls in my own set!). She had read more widely than I had believed it possible for a woman; those of my own family only read novels in the *Bons Livres* series. But what chiefly struck one about her was her judgment, and also something which she had in common with my mother, the wish and the will to lead and even to dominate. Balège, the shop assistant, used to say: 'What would the boss do without her? . . .'

It was on this occasion, after she had joined me under the arcades of the Grand Théâtre, where I had waited for her because of the rain, and when we were sitting in a café at the corner of the Rue Esprit-des-Lois, amidst that smell of absinthe which I loathed, that she told me in her downright, almost blunt manner what she felt I ought to know about her: 'As I've already told you, I couldn't possibly have any secret designs on you, or the sort of daydream that all girls have when they're in love and are loved . . .' Her father, a tax-collector in the Médoc (I remembered hearing the story) had deserted his wife, gambled, embezzled several million francs and been found hanged in a barn.

What could I do or say? Awkwardly, I took her hand, and she withdrew it. Then she added, deliberately: 'But I haven't finished,' in a neutral tone, as though giving evidence in Court about some sensational affair.

A friend of her parents had found her the job at Bard's. 'He was the same age as my father. He was good to us at first, but his feelings got the better of him and in the end I had to pay the price. He pestered me; my mother shut her eyes to it, and at that time I didn't care about anything. I never imagined what it was going to be like. I'm going to surprise you: I understand your mother better than you might think, not her worship of property but her loathing for the flesh. I'm so deeply grateful to you, above all, for not being like those beasts that pestered me. Even Balège, yes, that hunchback. He boasts of his successes, and he actually has some.'

So an old man had had her; she had agreed to that. I dared not look up at Marie. I asked, almost in a whisper: 'Who delivered you from him?'

'Angina pectoris. He was afraid of dying.'

Perhaps she was crying, but I could not see her eyes. I had chiefly a sense of embarrassment and distress. I repeated, in a strained voice: 'Don't cry.'

'I'm not crying for what I did, but because you've just called me *vous*.'

'Oh! I didn't mean to. Listen, Marie, I understand better now why you prefer me. You're a girl who has been thrown to the wild beasts and has escaped from them, and who'll always be afraid of them henceforward.'

She did not reply, she had something else to say to me, I could feel that. After a longish silence she made up her mind to it:

'Another thing that worries me is that you're a little Christian. Alain, am I going to sever you from that which is your life?'

I repeated: 'My life?' Her words surprised me; not because of the scruple they disclosed, but because of something forced about her tone of voice. I did not see this clearly at the time; it was an hour later, while I was slowly climbing the stair in the Rue de Cheverus, that I felt overwhelmed and then obsessed by the unease that she had awakened in me. This was not due to the religious difficulties she had referred to, but to the fact that she had suggested them; and suddenly, on the first floor landing that smelt of gas, as I paused to take breath, I said out loud: 'She was deceiving me.' It was another of my lightning-flash intuitions.

I fought against it. Surely this gift, which I was so proud of possessing, was something I had myself invented? or rather that Donzac had convinced me I had? I was crazy, to play such tricks on myself. I tried to reassure myself. I went back, point by point, over everything Marie had said to me in that café, and the motives and causes stood out clearly in a relentless light: it was obviously a pre-arranged conversation, so that I could learn from her own lips about the theft her father had committed, the whole sinister incident and what its sequel had been for her. Now no gossip could wound her; she was forearmed. She had no doubt expected a different reaction from me, once the blow had fallen. Why did she add that very un-expected comment: 'You're a little Christian . . .'

'A little Christian, a little Christian . . .' It meant, surely, that apart from marriage, which indeed she declared she had renounced, or rather of which she professed not to have thought, there could be nothing between us two. That was the thing of which she needed to convince me. I had answered lightheartedly that she should not worry on behalf of the little Christian, who would resign himself to being a sinner, as he was used to in his own way.

'No, Marie, don't concern yourself: *felix culpa!* If ever a sin was a blessed sin . . .'

And yet Marie was not mistaken: I had never cut myself off from the life of the sacraments; I could not bear the thought of that. It was strange that she should have guessed that. How did she know? How could a woman from that milieu, indifferent, as she must surely be, about religion, have concluded from the scanty information I had given her about myself on this subject, that participation in the sacraments was more necessary to me than unconsecrated bread and wine? It was not to be believed. She must have known it. She must have been told it by another person: by what other?

Oh, God! God! On that fateful landing, I could see it, dazzlingly clear. She had lied to me. Simon Duberc must have seen me, without my knowledge, in the bookshop and said to Marie: 'I know that poor student of yours, I know your angel.' They were in league. After all, she had no reason to know that I was one of those unhappy lads who think no woman can love them for their own sake. Had I ever confided in Simon on this matter? No . . . Yes, though! I remembered that I had told him about the wax model at the Bordeaux fair. 'He must have repeated that to her. And so she promptly stressed her own disgust. She's scheming against me, for sure.' Then I told myself: 'You've no proof! You're the victim of that Arabian story-teller that dwells inside you and invents endless stories to fill the gaps between the books you read, so that an unbroken wall may protect you from life. But this time the story you're telling yourself is really your own story. True or invented? How much is imaginary? Exactly where does it coincide with reality?'

I went through Mother's little drawing-room, which separates our two bedrooms. Although we have had electricity for the past two years I struck a match and lit the oil lamp, the same I had had since childhood, by the light of which I had read my books, learnt my lessons and prepared my exams. I sat down on the bed, my inward eye fixed on a set of facts about which I kept repeating: 'That proves nothing,' without convincing myself; yes, to be sure, Marie had carefully prepared her confession in the café, yes, she had hoped to kill two, even three birds with one stone, neutralizing beforehand anything I might learn about her past life, taking credit for seeming to have no secret thoughts of marriage, but at the same time reminding me of my sacramental life and declaring her resolve not to destroy it, so that if I could not do without Marie I should have to revert to the idea of marriage . . . Yes, but it was hardly probable that she should have any hope of that. And besides, the fact remained that she was attracted to me. I felt sure of that; I did not often attract people, but when I did, I knew it. I am never mistaken about desire in other people.

I noticed that the mail had been put on my bed: some newspapers, and one letter; it was from Mother. I took it under the lamp. I haven't the courage to copy it out. Why should I inflict it on Donzac? This sort of discussion cannot interest him. Mother was putting off her return for a few days. The game, she wrote, was well worth the candle. Numa Séris had decided against buying Tolose, which is by far the finest property in the arrondissement (it had been his turn to do business with her). 'He professes not to have the necessary capital. He's got it, of course, but he says to himself that he'll get Tolose in the end without spending a penny when you marry his daughter. He pays no attention to what I indicated of your aversion to the match. Evidently he does not suspect the strength of your antipathy. What's the point of telling him? We've at least ten years ahead of us. You may change. You will change . . .'

Nothing else existed – not even her pharisaical, fetishist religion, of which only the husk was left. Everything had been eaten away from within. But the inside had never existed. I looked round the room which was my room and bore no trace of me except for the books and journals. The paper was the same brown wallpaper that we had always had at home. 'Your grandmother adores brown.' All the objects reflected a Saint-Sulpice type religiosity: the worst sort of ugliness, due to a lack of culture.

I picked up from my desk the latest photographs of modern paintings that Donzac had sent me from Paris to 'educate my eye'. But how can one form any idea of a picture without colour? I had never seen any other canvas than *Tintoretto Painting his Dead Daughter* and *Everyone his Own Chimera* by Henri Martin, in the Bordeaux museum where we used to take shelter when it was raining.

I don't know why I thought about these depressing things just then, in that dead house where the only remaining vestige of life belonged to a couple of old servants asleep in an attic bedroom.

As usual when I am suicidally unhappy – and I say that literally, for as Donzac knows, many members of my family have taken their own lives – I knelt down by my bed and wept again, but this time with my forehead against an unseen shoulder. My whole religion lay in that gesture, like an unhappy child's, which to many others might seem both absurd and cowardly: as though it were cowardice for the stag at bay to take refuge in a pool from pursuing hounds! And I knew that a great peace would come over me, and that were I to live a hundred years, and even if all philosophers and learned men were to deny Christ, and even if nobody else was left with Him, I should still be there; not to serve others, like true Christians, not because I love others like myself, but only because I need that buoy so as to keep afloat, to stay on the surface of this atrocious world – so as not to founder.

This was the direction my thoughts took that evening, for as long as I stayed there kneeling with my face buried in the sheets. Deeply moved, I recalled a thought that had often been in my mind, even, at one period, soon after my first communion, to the point of obsession: the priesthood. But Mother had decreed that I lacked a vocation, and mobilized all the priests I knew to combat this whim of mine. Now I was twenty-one and nobody had any power over me. I would divest myself of everything at one blow. I would renounce my estates and leave them to Mother; she'd get them all, but it would kill her. For her mania was unbroken inheritance, inheritance triumphant over death. If I withdrew, there would only be some cousins . . . The State would swallow up everything. 'And in any case,' she'd conclude, 'the question doesn't arise. You've no vocation, that's as clear as daylight.' Everything that served the interests of her passion was beyond dispute, was as clear as daylight. But after all, I had only to go off without a backward look . . .

O God, passionately as I have loved my mother, it's not for her that I feel a love greater than my love for You. The resentment which I bear her is irremediably poisoned. The truth is that, like herself, I love Maltaverne better than I love You, but for other reasons than hers: I don't love these estates as such, nor possession in her sense of the word; I daren't confess this to anyone but Donzac. I cannot give up this land, these trees, this stream, the sky between the tops of the pine trees, those beloved giants, that scent of resin and marshland which – am I crazy? – is the very odour of my despair.

Such were my thoughts that evening. I tore off my clothes and flung myself, just as I was, into bed, and collapsed into sleep.

VI

When the breakfast tray was brought in next morning, when the curtains were drawn back to let in the pale autumnal sunshine, I was no longer the same desperate creature. I felt lucid and calm, and one clear idea had emerged from sleep and night: I knew what I had to do, or at least attempt to do. Marie had asked me to call just before the bookshop closed: at about six o'clock I would find Simon there – he would be arriving about then, so she assured me. But she had forgotten what she had told me earlier, that Simon Duberc spent the whole of his Thursday afternoons there, coming straight from Talence immediately after lunch. If I kept watch, I should therefore be able to waylay him before he went into the shop.

It was my one chance of finding out whether there had been a plot between Marie and himself and whether it was the plot I had imagined. Of course he would try to deceive me, but I knew he would not succeed. He was one of the few people over whom I have been granted power – I have been granted absolute power. I know that what I have written sounds mad; but I am writing for no one but Donzac who knows what I'm talking about; 'one of those whom you mesmerize . . .', as he says. I shall very soon learn everything, if I can spend half an hour with him elsewhere than in the street. But how can I be sure of meeting him? Coming from Talence by tram, he'll walk up the Rue Sainte-Catherine. 'I can't miss him if I keep watch from two o'clock onwards at the corner of the Rue Sainte-Catherine and the Galleries, unless they've decided to lunch together today to plan their campaign . . . No, she sometimes has dinner out but never lunch, because of her mother. She told me so; that's their arrangement, her mother prepares lunch . . .' So it must be at the bookshop that Simon was to meet her at two o'clock. I merely had to begin my watch early enough.

At half-past one I was standing at the entry to the Galleries, near the Rue Sainte-Catherine. The difficulty, in spite of the throng, was to pass unnoticed. I was obviously waiting for someone, but it might have been for no one in particular: a young person standing motionless on the pavement invites attention. I might have stared into shop-windows, but I could not risk missing Simon. I had an inordinate craving to see him and I refused to believe it would happen, because of a superstition that I have held since childhood that since things never take place as expected one must not picture them too clearly as one would like them to be.

It did happen, however; about three o'clock Simon suddenly crossed into my field of vision (he could not see me), walking with the stiff, upright gait I remembered, that formal imposing air he had acquired at the seminary, a peculiar stiff collar that might have been celluloid, and a broad-brimmed black felt hat – every inch a pedagogue. He had aged unbelievably. How old was he? Four years older than myself: twenty-five; it seemed hardly possible. In fact, the term 'ageless' seemed to apply to him in an absolute sense. It was suffering that had made him old, that uninterrupted suffering which had already lapped him as a child and which visibly submerged him today. Did I see all this at the time, at a first glance? No, I'm inventing it – and yet it must have been true. As long as I have known him, he always seemed to be immersed in some scalding liquid. What I am not inventing is the strange mineral texture of the planes of his face, as though fossilized. What I am not inventing is the sudden flush, when he saw me, of young blood into that petrified face, the flash of a smile, and then sudden panic: 'No, not now, Monsieur Alain, not yet,' he insisted, as I took his hand. I

hadn't been mistaken; he was anxious not to see me before we met
in the bookshop.

'Listen, Simon, I have to see you alone . . .'

'No, I've promised.'

'But you didn't know you would meet me. You were not responsible for this meeting; it was deliberately brought about . . .'

'You mean, by God? You're still the same, Monsieur Alain . . .
One's only got to look at you.'

'Brought about by God? I don't know. By myself, in any case.
I've been looking out for you for the past hour, and I'm not going
to let you go. You can tell Marie what you please, or you can tell
her nothing . . .'

Suddenly, at that moment, I was inspired to say the words he
expected:

'What does it matter to you and me? This business has nothing to
do with her. It's our own business, Simon, it concerns Maltaverne,
it's our secret . . .'

Once again a flush overspread his fossilized face. He repeated:
'Our secret, Monsieur Alain, our wretched secret . . .'

'Listen, do you know Prévost's chocolate shop? It's close by, along
the Allées de Tourny. There'll be nobody there just now. We can
stay as short a time as you like.'

He did not demur. We went along to the Place de la Comédie; he
talked, turning his head stiffly towards me. He told me that he had
no complaint to make about M. Duport, who had enabled him to
finish his second year's *licence* in Paris, and that thanks to M. Gaston
Doumergue he had been appointed to a junior post in Seine-et-Oise:
'But they hadn't reckoned with my accent. I'd never have imagined
the effect my accent would make in Paris, particularly on a class of
twelve-year-olds. I've often heard you say, "I only love trees,
animals and children"; well, I advise you to cut out the last item; you
don't know what children are capable of!' He had been ruthlessly

ragged: 'We don't know, in the Gironde, what a ridiculous impression we make as soon as we open our mouths.' Then he had been appointed to Talence: 'but even at Talence . . .' Marie had promised to help him. She knew a method. I told him there had been a great improvement and that his accent was no longer offensive. Did he ever go to Maltaverne?

'Good gracious no, I can't afford it. . . . No, it's not that so much. The truth is that Madame is there all the time, as you know. You mustn't even mention my name to her. And you must forgive me if I say I literally couldn't face seeing Madame. Not to speak of Mme Duport. She's never sober, and it frightens me. My parents came twice to Talence. I paid for their tickets. Prudent came once, he slept in my room, in my bed . . . You can imagine . . .'

We went into Prévost's. There were, as I had foreseen, only a couple of people there, lunching off a cup of chocolate. 'It must remind you of your tea-time snacks at Mme Duport's,' I teased him. But he never laughed; he seemed immune to irony, mistrustful and prickly. He buttered his bread with care, dipped it in his chocolate, and ate voraciously, saying nothing. Time was running short.

'It's odd that Marie tried to deceive me,' I said. 'Why did she conceal the fact that you had spoken of me, that you'd told her all about me . . .'

'She's a girl who only tells what she wants to tell . . .'

'And she's got some plan in the back of her mind about me. Yes, after all, I'm a good match.'

'Oh, I say! She's not that crazy! The Gajac son and heir, and a shop-assistant! Not to speak of her reputation. No, she's too intelligent . . . And besides she knows you, though she did let fall one day (don't let her know I told you): "I could have your angel if I wanted him . . ." I even believe she said: "I can have him when I want him." But that might just have meant . . .'

He was talking with his mouth full of bread and chocolate. I said: 'Now I'm out of the trap.'

'What trap? There isn't any trap. She loves you, didn't you know? I was jealous enough, I bore you a grudge . . . No, that's not true, I bore you no grudge. At heart I've always felt that you were entitled to everything. Well then, let's say we just met at the corner of the Rue Sainte-Catherine and the Galleries, after all it's the truth. What we won't tell her is this talk we've been having at Prévost's . . .'

I paid, and stood up. It was barely five minutes' walk to the book-shop.

'She won't believe us,' I said suddenly, 'any more than I believed her. You're lying to both of us, Simon. I can understand your lying to her, but to me!'

He muttered: 'I mean nothing to you, do I?' I made no reply. As we were going into the Galleries we decided at the last minute to give up all pretence and let Marie know the truth about our meeting. We had barely crossed the threshold of the shop, which had its usual Thursday throng of customers, when she saw us, swept a swift, intense glance over us, and without responding to our smiles returned to the customers who were harassing her. We stood there beside the window. Simon said to me: 'She'll never forgive me, any more than she can forgive herself for concealing the fact that she knew all about you thanks to me. All the same, it's true that she liked you when she thought you were poor.'

Just then she had a moment's respite and came up to us. This time she smiled, and made as if to send us out.

'Now that you've met again you've no reason to be here. I'd only be in your way.'

When I protested that we would come back and fetch her when the shop closed, she curtly forbade that. She was speaking to both of us, but in fact she looked only at me. I alone existed. She touched my forehead with her finger: 'God knows what's going on inside there,' she said, 'the things you'll invent . . . Well, it can't be helped! In any case M. Duberc has nothing to tell you about me, for he knows nothing about me.'

A customer snapped her up. I thought Simon had not heard her words, but as soon as we were outside the door he exclaimed furiously:

'Oh, so I know nothing about her? I know far more than she imagines, and I know what she's desperately anxious to hide from you, and thinks I've no conception of . . .'

I have all too often been the one of two men whom a woman does not look at, and I never felt more than a vague jealousy, none of that bitterness to which Simon now gave vent, almost despairingly, because, so he thought, it would always be like this for him: 'I'm doomed to *la mère* Duport . . . Goodbye . . .' I grasped his arm and asked him to go back with me to the Rue de Cheverus: 'You can rest in my room for a moment . . .' He followed me, but unwillingly, hanging his head. What did he know? What had he insinuated about Marie? I was not distressed. I wanted to know! to have everything made clear about her. It was a detached and almost indifferent curiosity. But I had let slip the moment when Simon might have spoken out of vindictiveness. I must not take any risks. He was greatly impressed by our staircase, which he climbed with almost religious awe.

'Yes,' I said, 'the staircase isn't bad. They knew how to build at Bordeaux, two hundred years ago . . . But the rooms! What we've made of them!'

I had taken him into the drawing-room where Mounestet, my mother's upholsterer, had dressed up the windows, as he said, with an abundance of loops, tassels, fringes and tufts, which dazzled Simon:

'It's splendid.'

'It's hideous. Think of your kitchen at home, Simon, the Duberc kitchen, with hams hanging from the beams, and the rustic clock beating like the heart of the place, and the dresser, and the homely earthenware dishes and the tin spoons and forks and the smell of flour and goose-fat, but above all of that holy dimness in which God dwells, that of the pilgrims of Emmaus . . .'

'Why, good gracious, you seem to believe what you're saying!'

'A bourgeois home like ours is absolute ugliness. As soon as a peasant begins to rise in the world and thinks about having a drawing-room, he goes in for something that's bourgeois and therefore hideous.'

Simon kept repeating: 'Why, good gracious!'

I took him into my mother's little parlour.

'So this is where Madame lives!' he said in a tone of mingled reverence and hatred.

'She doesn't live here very much now. Just imagine, Simon, what my life is like in this old dead house. We live only in one wing of it. But I admit that I myself am responsible for creating this desert. I have always been afraid of other people . . .'

'Specially of girls?'

'Not more than of boys.'

'But not of Marie? She says she's taming you . . .' He gave that brief tight-lipped smile that I remembered from his childhood.

'What is it that you know about her, Simon, that she doesn't know that you know . . .'

'Oh, Monsieur Alain, forget what I let slip just now when I was so angry. It would be wrong to tell you . . . And yet,' he added, 'it might help you to understand her. She hasn't told you all about herself, but what she's kept from you might perhaps make her dearer to you, or perhaps more hateful . . . How is one to know with you?'

'Who can have spoken to you about her at Talence? And here you don't know anyone. I don't believe you.'

'All right, then, don't believe me. I never asked you . . .' He had stiffened.

'But I'm asking you, Simon, to tell me everything. Help me, since you know what would make her dearer or more hateful to me. You can't leave me in suspense. What am I going to imagine now?'

My anguish was genuine, but at the same time I exaggerated it so as to overcome Simon's lingering reluctance. He could see real tears on my cheeks, although perhaps I should not have shed them had I been alone. That's what I am like, God forgive me.

There was nothing mysterious about the accident through which Simon had found out what he knew. The bookshop assistant, Balège, lived in the Saint-Genès district, and went home by tram every evening. As the same tram also went on to Talence, Simon happened to be on it one Thursday evening after the shop shut; and they fell into conversation.

'That hunchback's another who's obsessed by Marie. He lives alone without relatives or friends, and I'm the first living soul to whom he's been able to pour out his feelings about Marie, and who has listened to him with interest and, as he's gathered, with a passion equal to his own.'

I am not going to retail for Donzac's benefit all that Simon told me; I'm not going to reconstruct the scene, giving it the false authenticity of a 'narrative'. All Donzac needs to know is that when I learned of the extreme misfortunes which had afflicted Marie and from which she was still suffering, I felt a sense of relief, that I have breathed more freely from that moment. Now I understand, from what Simon learned from Balège, the reasons for the premonition which she seemed to have had of the scruples and inner needs of a practising Christian like myself. There had been, at any rate to begin with, no thought of blackmailing me into marriage, when she re- minded me of my Christian observances and my devotion to the sacraments. It needed only the picture sketched by Simon of my pious childhood, of my mother and her Spanish-type religion, of the stifling atmosphere of Maltaverne, for this girl, with her boundless gifts of intuition and understanding, to appreciate my experience, since it was paralleled by her own. Her father had been a dissolute official; her mother was a woman of considerable piety, of a sort apparently more enlightened than my own mother's. An eminent cleric, of whom I shall say nothing that might enable Donzac to identify him definitely, used to spend every summer at Soulac-sur-mer, where Marie's family lived. He became the spiritual director of the two women. Marie acted as his willing secretary and favourite disciple. She owed to him her love of ideas, her culture, so unexpected in a provincial girl; and at that period, according to Balège, she had given herself heart and soul to the Church, so she believed, but in fact to this man.

I have indeed no reason to believe Simon's possibly distorted version of Balège's gossip. I need only to understand that the sudden tragic ebbing of faith from a soul that had been totally immersed in it must have been, in Marie's case, linked with the discovery (made by many young Christians) that the saint in whom they had placed implicit trust was himself only a poor creature of flesh and blood like any other, worse than others because of the mask he was doomed to wear. Disconverted by the man who had converted them . . . yes, I have known several such. But I'm going too far; I am inventing what I have just insinuated. All I know for sure in this affair is that after the scandal of her father's suicide Marie had to give up her post in the youth organization of which this cleric was a patron, and that this caused her much suffering, that the friend who introduced her to Bard's, and who was himself a fanatical disciple of the priest, quarrelled with him about her. As to what really happened, Balège has no proof. Even if nothing took place between these two middle-aged men, one of whom was entirely under the influence of the other, beyond what might flare up in a bar or in the street between two boys quarrelling over a girl, I fancy that's enough to account for Marie's present hostility to religion and at the same time her understanding, her actual experience of my personal problem . . .

'And you too, Simon,' I said, 'and I myself, must suffer as she has done from the fact that the word of the Son of Man, the Son of God, can only come to us through sinners. But not only His Word. He identifies Himself with them. That's the reason for the failure which has been going on for two thousand years.'

'Monsieur Alain, you've kept your faith.'

'And you, Simon, do you think you have lost yours?'

He made no reply, but hid his face for a moment in his two misshapen hands. He sighed:

'What does it mean, having faith? What does losing it mean? I thought I had lost it. M. Duport got a friend of his, a teacher at the Sorbonne, to draw up a synoptic table for me of all the reasons why it's impossible that God should exist. Don't laugh; you know nothing about modern science, Monsieur Alain, and nor do I . . .'

'But there's something else that's impossible for you and me: that there should not have been, at a certain moment, someone who said certain things . . .'

'Who's supposed to have said certain things.'

'Yes, and done certain things.'

'We're the last people to attach any importance to that. You have never been out in the world, Monsieur Alain. If you only knew how little all that counts for in Paris, how it's all ancient history . . .'

'But you and I know that it exists.'

'What d'you mean by "it"? What they've dinned into you since your childhood, what I've had stuffed down my throat since my schooldays?'

'No, Simon on the contrary, something that lives on in spite of these formulae and conventions, in spite of our training, something which is unconnected with the mechanical side of us . . . But you understand; you're the only person who can understand me!'

He asked me, in a low voice, with repressed fervour: 'What makes you believe that?'

But what is the use of offering Donzac a conversation which has been rearranged and touched up, and the essential part of which, moreover, was inspired by himself? I should like to isolate, to detach from its context the thing that mattered in that evening's encounter, that may perhaps have changed my life, that has made it for ever different from what it would have been if that ghost, Simon, had not reappeared . . . Or rather, I should say: the thing that prevented my life from changing when Marie was about to divert its course, that made the heathland stream return to its bed between the alders, those incorruptible guardians . . . I am sure that it was that evening, and not later, that Simon made me capable of facing my mother as an enemy, for it was in that little parlour in the Rue de Cheverus that he opened my eyes: and he never went back there subsequently, for my mother returned from Maltaverne two days later, after her purchase of Tolose.

Henceforward I went to Bard's every Thursday at four o'clock. Simon waited for me there. Marie, surrounded by customers, would smile at me from afar. Simon and I went out together, to Prévost's; I avoided sitting opposite him, so as not to see him dip his buttered croissant into his chocolate. We went back to meet Marie after the bookshop closed, not in her favourite café at the corner of the Rue Esprit-des-Lois (we had become more prudent since my mother's return) but in the chilly parlour in the Rue de l'Eglise-Saint-Seurin.

But first I must let Donzac know what Simon had told me that evening, when he came to the Rue de Cheverus. He had learnt the secret from his brother Prudent, when the latter paid his one and

only visit to Talence. My mother was not as convinced as I had
believed of my submission and of her final victory. At twenty-one I
was liable to fall a prey to the first-comer of either sex. The risk was
that some fortune-hunter might get hold of me. My aversion to
marriage no longer reassured her, because she realized that marriage
was my only certain defence against the Louse. The dangerous years,
she thought, were those of my student life at Bordeaux. She knew
that I was no easy prey. She was aware of the *vis inertiae* with which
I met any attempt to seduce me. But a chance encounter might well
bring out another side of me: a man like other men, worse than
other men. So long as I had not come back to Maltaverne, come back
to stay, nothing would have been won. When she had finally got
me back, when I should have cast anchor there for ever, then all
that she had planned could be achieved.

The important thing, as she explained to old Duberc (it was from
him that Prudent had learnt the secret that he told his brother) was
not to let oneself be taken by surprise. 'He's slipped my grasp,' she
kept on saying. 'I've lost control over him.' If I decided to marry,
the worst thing, in Mother's view, would be that I should make a
conventionally acceptable choice which no one could criticize. But
even then she would be able to raise insuperable objections: they are
always to be found. I should have to submit to her veto, which
would be absolute. She derived all her strength from my incapacity
to manage my own affairs or even give serious thought to them. In
spite of my success at school, in which she gloried on prize-giving
day, she judged me according to that scale of values which was
current in her family: it was identical with that of Père Grandet.
Nothing has changed in France since Balzac's day. 'A poor creature',
that's what I was for Mother, in spite of all my book-learning.

If I proved obstinate, she would retire to her estate at Noaillan,
and leave me to cope with my two thousand hectares by myself.
Worse still, in order to foil me completely she had secured the

Dubercs' promise to follow her to Noaillan, so that I should have no alternative but to submit, being unable to do without my bailiff as well as my mother. It would be for my own good, she would save me in spite of myself. I could imagine her saying it: 'I've looked after you and I shall go on looking after you to the end of my days.'

Simon had begun by speaking in a detached tone, and as though fulfilling a duty: 'I think you ought to know, Monsieur Alain . . .' But a resentment which had been building up since early childhood against 'Madame' gradually filtered through every word he said. As for my own reaction . . . Even in her absence Mother could still strike me with a kind of stupor. She had me in her grasp, and she was well aware of it. I sighed: 'There's no solution.'

'Yes, there is, Monsieur Alain, there is a solution. It was Marie's idea. She'll set you free if you're willing.'

He stubbornly refused to tell me anything about it; it was for Marie and not for him to explain the plan she had conceived. Suddenly, after a silence, he said with muffled passion: 'As for me I swear to you, Monsieur Alain, that if ever you found yourself without a bailiff or anybody, well, you know that I know the way about the estate as well as my father. Just give me a sign and I'll be with you. Oh, don't think I'd be sacrificing everything for your sake; I'd gladly give up the hell of my life at Talence to be back at Maltaverne . . .'

'And Maltaverne means myself.'

He turned his head away, and got up. 'Till Thursday then, at the bookshop.'

I heard the sound of Simon's footsteps growing fainter down the staircase, then the heavy door clanged. I emerged from my stupor, which was partly assumed, or at any rate which was what I displayed whenever Mother came into the picture. But that evening when I was alone I indulged in a sort of cold fury which was directed not against her alone, but against Marie who had dared to make a plan: *the rage of one who is considered a weakling and who arouses women's compassion, whereas inwardly he is overflowing with infinite power. 'I'll show them! I'll show them!' What would I show them? The important thing was to keep a cool head. The best thing I had learnt that evening was that Simon would throw up everything at my first summons. 'To escape from his hell', he had said. Maybe . . . But he'd do it for nobody else. Whatever happened, I should not be alone.

VII

My mother came back from Maltaverne two days later, still reeking of the battle she had waged over the purchase of Tolose: a hundred hectares of pine and oak forest, five kilometres away from the village. Numa Séris had considered the price excessive. She herself was convinced of having made a good investment. After dinner we sat down by the fireside in her little drawing-room. I asked her, with the casual inattentive manner I assume when such matters are involved, where she had found the money for the purchase of Tolose.

'Oh, it came from my permanent reserve fund.'

'Yes; from this year's mine-props and resin harvest. Not to mention the pines you've had cut in the Brousse . . .'

She glanced at me. I had my usual absent-minded expression, which no doubt reassured her.

'What matters,' she said, 'is to have the money, not to know where it comes from.'

'But it matters to me. If you paid for Tolose out of your personal income from Noaillan, it belongs to you. If it was out of the income from Maltaverne . . .'

She flushed. 'What are you thinking of? You know our interests are identical.'

'But they're not identical with the interests of the State. It would really be too bad to have to pay death duties on the Tolose estate, which in fact belongs to me. And besides, our interests are not always identical; I've taken no vows of celibacy.'

I took care not to break the ensuing silence. It lasted a long time,

or so it seemed to me. Then Mother said in a low voice: 'Somebody's
been working on you. Who is it?'

I assumed an air of the utmost surprise. I reminded Mother that I
was now twenty-one, that I was quite capable of asking myself
certain questions. Then she broke out into denunciations of my in-
gratitude: she had managed our affairs with a prudence and success
that were recognized everywhere as exemplary, she had increased
our fortunes beyond belief; she would retire to Noaillan if I wished
it and have nothing more to do with my affairs. I remained unmoved
by these threats; I nodded gently, and even smiled. Mother left the
little parlour, went up to her bedroom and bolted the door, following a familiar pattern whose sequence, this time, I was determined to
break: I would not go to knock at her door as usual, pleading: 'Let
me in, Maman!'

I threw a log on the fire and sat there motionless, in a state of calm
despair which was the very reverse of that peace of God of which, at
certain times, I had a presentiment. But every day I was drifting
further away from that; or rather 'this world's goods' seemed to
spin an ever thicker cocoon around me, who set myself up as im-
placable judge against my mother, whereas the two of us were
contesting for the possession of the land, which belongs to everyone
and to no one, and which will in turn possess us.

This time she was not going to win. Mother would never win
again. Perhaps she sensed this. I remembered her exclamation:
'somebody's been working on you!' She must have questioned
Louis Larpe and his wife about my doings, the minute she returned;
she always did. The dinner ordered for a lady friend and then
counter-ordered an hour later by the lady herself was more than
enough to upset Mother. I had proof of this next moment; I heard
the bolt of her door being drawn back. She had not waited for me to
ask her pardon, but was taking the first step herself. She sat down in
front of me again as if nothing had happened between us.

'I've thought it over, Alain. It's true that I keep forgetting you are grown up, and treat you too much like the small boy you used to be. I tried to relieve you of everything, to keep you uninvolved. That was what you wanted. But what a joy it would be if you'd at last consent to take an interest in the duties that belong to your position! You won't always have me with you.'

She broke off, assuming that I would get up and kiss her, but I remained motionless and silent. She then reminded me that until Laurent's death she had not bought an acre of land or made the slightest investment except as our guardian and in both our names. Since we had lost Laurent, and up till the purchase of Tolose, only unimportant plots of land had been involved. About Tolose she had had to act quickly, as the seller was threatening to change his mind. She had been obliged to sign the deed and pay out the money that same day, but she admitted that she had been wrong to act so hastily. She would do all that was needed and would pay back the price of Tolose into the Maltaverne account, out of her own property.

'And if you ever marry, Tolose shall be my wedding present. But young men don't get married at twenty-one.'

'Because they're in the army. That's been spared me, too; I shall have dodged everything. Perhaps I shan't dodge marriage.'

'I should hope not.'

I gave no word, no sign of agreement; the silence between us became intolerable. We rose and wished one another goodnight.

It had not yet struck ten. I reflected that each of us, in our separate rooms, must be preoccupied with the same person: for Mother, this was the unknown creature whom I had invited one evening in her absence and who had altered me to such an extent that I had called her to account about Tolose; but for me, too, this was an unknown woman, although I had held her in my arms for a few moments and had believed that she loved me; she had lied to me, she knew that I knew it and she had as yet made no attempt to find out what was going on inside me . . .

Since meeting Simon I had not been back to the bookshop; that was three days ago. Marie must have interpreted this as a hostile verdict, and yet she had put up no resistance. The wild ringdove she had tamed had taken fright and flown off; she would try to forget me. This was the reaction I ascribed to her. And then I remembered what Simon had told me of Marie's plan to save me from marriage with the Louse. Marie's plan, conceived by Marie.

I had resolved to lie low until Thursday, when we were to meet Simon. But next day, on my way back from the University, I could hold out no longer. I tried to resist. I paused, as I did almost every day, at the Cathedral, which is on my way home: indeed, the quickest way home was through the Cathedral. I often lingered there. It was the place in all the world where I felt most sheltered from the world, immersed, as it were, in that boundless love from which I was cut off for ever, like that rich young man who 'went away sorrowful, for he was one that had great possessions'.

That day I did not linger. I went up the Rue Sainte-Catherine as far as the Galeries Bordelaises. Marie saw me before I had even crossed the threshold of the bookshop; and I saw at the first glance that she had been suffering. It had aged her. She was no longer a young girl, nor even a young woman; she was someone who had suffered for years, but who was now suffering because of me. There's a streak in my nature, as Donzac knows, which may be common to other men or may be very peculiar: when I am fond of anyone I need their suffering for reassurance. I immediately had a sense of great peace, before we had exchanged a single world. We merely clasped hands furtively. I told her to meet me at Prévost's as soon as she was free, and I spent the interval wandering like a stray dog through the maze of forlorn streets in the Saint-Michel and Sainte-Croix districts. Then I waited for her at Prévost's, sitting before my cup of chocolate in sheer physical enjoyment of rest. She came in at last. She had 'put on rouge', as Mother would have said censoriously.

'I've not come to justify myself. You can believe what you like . . . But not that my motives were shameful. I knew that if you saw Simon Duberc and I was not there, our story would be ended before it had begun . . .'

'I lied to you too, Marie. We deceived one another so as not to lose one another.'

'One cannot lose what one has never had. No, Alain, I haven't lost you.'

She had not lost me, but she wanted to save me. She thought me in mortal danger, if it means death for a man to be tied against his will to a woman who repels him as much as the Louse would repel me. My mother knew that time was on her side, that each year that passed would bring her nearer to the realization of a dream she had cherished every instant of her life.

'We must forestall her, now that we know which way she'll attack . . . But first of all, Alain, since it all depends on you, you've got to know yourself whether you're with us in our efforts to set you free. Simon Duberc tells me you're sure of it. Perhaps you were sure on the evening you met, and perhaps you're less sure today?'

She tried to meet my eyes, but as we were sitting side by side I found it easy to avert them. I told her that I was sure of everything and yet of nothing, that I would never resume a yoke which I had already cast off in my mind, but that I reserved judgment as to the methods which were being offered me.

I don't quite know how it happened that, after that, our talk was chiefly about Simon Duberc. She spoke to me about him freely and, I think, with no ulterior motive, and what she told me made sense of

Simon's offer to drop everything in order, not so much to follow
me, as to escape from 'the hell of Talence'. Poor Simon. His hell was
inside himself. In Paris he had been on the verge of suicide. He still
was, and the only thing that kept him back was a lingering vestige of
religious faith, which had preserved him against all the attempts of
his new masters to make use of him. They had suggested a book:
the confessions of a peasant boy, led astray from his true vocation
by a rich *dévote*. The plan of the book would have been provided for
him, and he would merely have had to fill the pigeon-holes. Simon
demurred, and no pressure was put on him; since they were pleased
with him in the secretariat he was allowed to have his way . . . I
suddenly burst forth: 'So it was to talk about Simon that I've waited
for you for two hours and more this afternoon, wandering miserably
about this maze of sinister streets . . .'

'Yes, it's quite true that I'm talking about him because I dare not
talk to you about yourself, because I know what you're going to
think . . . but how could you think such a thing? You know whose
daughter I am, you know how much older I am than yourself
and what I've done with my time, or rather what other people
have done to me during that time – what some old men have done
to me. Oh, what I was like at your age, Alain, what I was like
then . . .'

If she was acting at that moment, what an actress she was! The
thing that must have hurt her most was my silence. I uttered no
protest, because the words that my decent upbringing suggested
then, the only ones that came into my mind, would have been
crueller than abuse.

She had to convince me, she said, that she had nothing to gain by
evolving this plot except the sort of pleasure one finds in releasing a
fly before the spider has devoured it. At last she set out her plan of
campaign: next time my mother went to Maltaverne I should write
to tell her of my engagement to 'the girl from Bard's bookshop'.

Marie would agree to my using her, as being precisely the sort of woman that would most appal my mother: her background, her age, what Mother would quickly discover about Marie's family and about her past, would be more than enough to make her issue an ultimatum; and as I should stand firm, she would then withdraw to her estate at Noaillan, taking the Dubercs with her.

Here I interrupted Marie; it seemed to me incredible that the Dubercs could be detached from Maltaverne, to which they clung like an oyster to its shell. According to Marie, there was nothing to be feared on that score; old Duberc would know it was merely a ruse to prevent me from falling into the clutches of a temptress from the city. Like his mistress, he dreamed of reigning one day over the lands of Numa Séris, and he thought himself irreplaceable. He was convinced that after one week I should send for him.

I asked, after a pause: 'Do you think she won't parry the blow? You don't know my mother.'

'I know you, Alain. Her strength lies in your weakness. You're master of the whole situation. Everything is in your power, but you are in hers.'

I made no protest. Marie rose, and left by herself. It would not have done for us to be seen together. We agreed to meet on Thursday at the bookshop, with Simon.

Although I was not late back for dinner, Mother was waiting for me on the landing. I could see her long pale face bent over the banister: 'Oh, there you are.' She would not go away, she'd keep her eye on me; that would be her first line of defence. Now Marie's plan, I felt, could not be realized unless Mother were away at Maltaverne. It must be by letter that she learned of my engagement. I should never dare to tell her face to face; if I attempted to, I should very soon be unmasked. I had never lied to her without being promptly made to feel ashamed.

All winter, without having me spied on or shadowed in any way, she knew that every Thursday, when I came home, I had been in conclave with her unknown enemies. On those evenings when Marie sat waiting for me behind her door in the Rue de l'Eglise Saint-Seurin and took me into the icy parlour, and when, on my return, however late it was, I went to give my mother the compulsory, ritual goodnight kiss, even though I stopped to wash my face and hands at the kitchen sink my mother would draw me to her, sniffing, recognizing an unfamiliar smell about my person. Not that she ever said anything about it. I knew that she knew. We were atrociously transparent to one another.

Moreover, that winter she had an irrefutable proof that I was deceiving her. Although I detested dancing, I would accept all invitations without a murmur, and almost every evening I'd put on my dinner jacket or my tail coat. Before I left, Mother would say: 'You must tell me all about it . . .' and when I got back she would cross-examine me. She wanted to know all about the party and she quickly guessed that I knew nothing about it because I had not gone, or had stayed only a moment; and it was easy enough to check up on this. I never put in more than a fleeting appearance at these dances. A further proof was that she no longer saw me take Communion, for I managed never to attend Mass at the same time as herself. Even at Christmas I was invited by a friend to a party in the country.

Louis Larpe always brought the mail to Mother, and she sorted it herself. There were never any suspicious letters for me. She did not pick up Marie's trail, nor Simon's. We never went out together; we had given up meeting at Prévost's, or at Marie's café at the corner of the Rue Esprit-des-Lois. We met either at the bookshop after closing hours in Marie's 'den', or in the parlour in the Rue de l'Eglise Saint-Seurin. Since it was out of the question for Simon to return to the Rue de Cheverus, I would sometimes go to visit him at

Talence myself, in fine weather. He was lodging with a widow in one of those bungalows that the Bordelais call *échoppes*. For a long time he had refused to let me visit him there: such is the incredible gulf that lies between different classes, with the consent of the poor and often against the will of those rich people who are ashamed of their wealth, as I was.

It was a commonplace room, with mahogany furniture, overlooking a presbytery garden, and beyond that the Bayonne road. Everywhere there were journals and books: not fiction or poetry but Boutroux's *Pascal*, the autobiography of St Teresa, *Saint Francis of Assisi* by Joergensen, St John of the Cross . . . He told me on my first visit, as I expressed surprise at these books: 'Thanks to you, I'm renewing my religious education', and then changed the subject. I became aware, that first day, how vital for him was the fulfilment of that dream: the two of us together at Maltaverne. It was a crazy dream, and yet one that could be realized.

Although he was the most impatient of the three, he did not think that Marie was right to want to take immediate action or to make me insist on going off by myself to Paris or Nice, whence I could write to my mother to announce my engagement. It seemed to Simon very important that the bomb should explode when my mother was at Maltaverne, which was only a few kilometres away from Noaillan, so that her prompt and spectacular removal with the Dubercs could take place at once. We should not have to wait long; in spite of her determination not to leave me alone, my mother would have to go to Maltaverne to see about the sale of resin and mine-props and to count the pines in various cuttings.

We had not foreseen that with the De Dion she could leave at dawn and be back in Bordeaux the same evening. Twice she went over to Maltaverne for a single night, but she never spent any length of time there. My twenty-second year went by in this fashion; and meanwhile, by imperceptible degrees, Marie made of the youthful angel a being like other men; but the child in me survived these actions, and reappeared, as soon as they were accomplished, not indeed to curse Marie but to cling to her, letting himself be lulled.

At least it was some consolation, that year, to see Simon become less hopeless. He envisaged his life at Maltaverne as a retreat where he and I, whether I were present or absent, would together seek, and end by finding – what? He said I had shed light for him on the evident truth that almost everything about the Church that its enemies hated was in fact hateful, and had always been so, at every moment of man's history: such as Madame's pharisaical religion. These enemies attacked structures which others worshipped, as Huysmans, for instance, adored Gregorian chant; and such adoration was as vain as their curses. We knew, he and I, that at a certain moment of history God had revealed Himself and still revealed Himself in the individual lives of certain men and women whose common feature was their close devotion to the Cross.

'That's forbidden to you, Monsieur Alain, because you are the rich young man. But not to me. I'm poor and I shall remain poor. You must not give me a penny more than Madame gives my father. I shall further benefit by those flashes of light which are granted you, those inspirations.'

I warned him against the illusion that any infallible ways exist to reach God consciously; I reminded him that nothing in the world is less dependent on our own will, and that our desire for it betrays a spiritual greed as reprehensible as that from which we had sought to escape.

So nothing happened. As it was my second year at the University, preparation for the *licence* served as an alibi for all my problems.

Marie and Simon adjusted their plan of campaign to the oppor-
tunities offered by the summer holidays. They could not conceive
how a young man of twenty-two could be reluctant to travel without his mother, not merely because of the resentment she would feel
but because he was himself still the same child who was liable to
panic when his mother left him alone in the carriage for a moment
while she went to buy a newspaper: on a journey even more than in
everyday life, she relieved him of all responsibilities. But she had
never helped me in my studies as Marie did during that period before
the written examination, when I spent every evening with her in the
Rue de l'Eglise Saint-Seurin after the bookshop had closed. I had
persuaded my mother to have dinner served later.

A year went by like this; we had meant it to be dramatic, and it
was uneventful, except for what went on inside each one of us, and
about that, even in my own case, anything I could say would be
invented, or arranged for Donzac's benefit. I think my spirit was
quiescent, that my studies for the examination had made me put
everything else on one side. I avoided any self-questioning about
Marie, because she was unhappy.

And even God . . . Here again Donzac will recognize his own
influence. He used to assert that nature must sometimes be granted a
holiday. I knew that Marie was sad because everything must come
to an end between us two, but she had retained from the time when
she worked for Father X . . . the recollection of a certain mystic's
doctrine about 'the sacrament of the present moment'. She would
say to me: 'This instant has been granted me, you are here, I am
here, I'm not looking beyond.'

Not that during this period I did not sometimes feel uneasy about
Marie. She had lied to me, and she might lie to me again. I imagined
her quite capable of playing the part of a victim suffering because of
me, the victim that I needed in order not to suffer myself. Perhaps
she had not disclosed her whole plan to me. Perhaps it included

schemes known to her alone, perhaps I should find myself some day bound to her for all time and for all eternity. But I was on my guard, I should not be taken by surprise, she would only hold me as long as I was willing . . . Of the three of us, only Simon was overflowing with hope.

VIII

It was at the time when we might least have expected it that everything began to happen. In July I passed my *licence* with distinction. As I refused to accompany Mother to Dax, where she was to go for a cure, she gave up her trip so as not to let me out of her sight, and we were left face to face, hardly speaking to one another beyond the necessary minimum, in the intolerable August heat of Maltaverne, under its fiery sky; we became like night birds that only leave their hiding-place at dusk.

Marie, tied to her bookshop, wept as she said good-bye to me, but a crazy scheme suggested by Simon gave her the courage, so she said, to go on living in a Bordeaux from which I was absent. She would soon see me again, and she would at last discover Maltaverne.

My mother had resigned herself to keeping the promise she had long ago made to the old Dubercs, to take them with her to Lourdes on the diocesan pilgrimage of August 17 to 20. What delighted but terrified the Dubercs was that the journey was to be made in the De Dion; Louis Larpe and his wife being on holiday, I should be left alone at Maltaverne with Prudent (who, however, was our accomplice), looked after by Prudent's wife, whom he had married last January, a scared and servile creature who would undoubtedly hold her tongue if he gave the order. All the bourgeois homes of the village would be empty; their inhabitants had either flocked to Lourdes after M. le Doyen like so many old sheep, or else were on holiday in the hills or by the sea.

Marie and Simon were to stay with the Dubercs. We looked no further. As for what would happen between us, and then with my

Mother on her return, I refused to think about it. I was well aware
that Mother, for her part, as the time for her departure drew nearer,
was anxious about leaving me alone at Maltaverne. Why should I
not spend those three days at Luchon, she suggested, and she would
then join me there after handing over the Dubercs to M. le Doyen?
I must have refused with a harshness that offended her but above all
warned her, as I realize today, that something was in the wind. I
pretended to be looking forward to my lonely stay in a Maltaverne
unexpectedly drained of human life. She had stopped accusing me of
talking nonsense; she watched me, wondering what my crazy talk
might conceal.

'What will you do during these three days?'

'I shall walk. I'll go and see the old man of Lassus again, to find
out what I shall be like in sixty years' time, when I'm the old man of
Maltaverne.'

I was terrified that Mother might change her mind and think of
some pretext for not going. I only breathed freely once I heard the
noise of the De Dion's engine grow fainter along the road and when,
alone on the terrace, I rapturously breathed in the misty morning air
that heralded a torrid day, a day of endless waiting. Simon and
Marie were to arrive by the evening train. Prudent was to go alone
to meet them at the station and would bring them back to Maltaverne by a short cut through the woods, which was always deserted
at night.

Prudent's wife cleaned out his parents' room thoroughly and laid
the best sheets on the bed. I told her to prepare the guest room in the
château (as she called our house) just in case the lady found it more
convenient, since it had a *cabinet de toilette*. She obeyed, with no
expression of surprise.

About that evening and that night I should not like to write anything resembling those narratives that aroused André Donzac's

jealousy in our schooldays. And yet that witness to my life must be told that this was the moment that gave my life its meaning, because it was a night of sin and yet a night of grace.

I had taken her suitcase and led the way into the guest room without asking her opinion or Simon's. In her light summer dress, with her straw hat, she was a different creature from the Marie in the bookshop; this was the girl I had not known, but that others had known. It was a brief pang.

The three of us met in the dining-room for a quick and silent meal. It was she who asked me to take her round the park. She paused on the terrace. I threw my old school cloak over her shoulder. She walked slowly down the steps. She said to me: 'I know it all already, thanks to you. It's all just like you.' I told her that if she had been disappointed I could not have forgiven her.

The only pines she knew were those at Soulac, by the side of which our Maltaverne pines were giants. I held her arm to guide her along the avenue. 'Is that the big oak tree?' She had recognized it, although it was like many another oak tree; I pressed my lips to it, according to the rite, and then Marie and I exchanged our first kiss.

'What I love so much about Maltaverne . . .' On this theme I was inexhaustible, and Marie had already heard often enough of my aversion to conventional beauty spots, and how the only natural scenes that moved me were those that appealed to myself alone and to those who loved them through me and in me. We did not go as far as the stream because the meadow would have been wet, but we stood motionless and speechless, listening to that furtive purling that went on and on and would go on for endless centuries to come.

'Why is it,' I asked Marie, 'that something which I never feel at the edge of great rivers or even of the sea is conveyed to me by this stream in which as a child I used to sail the boats I had carved out of pine-tree bark?' To know that one is ephemeral is not the same as feeling it in one's bones. That was what one small boy learned from the purling of the Hure, on those summer nights long ago when he paused to listen to the silence, that silence alive with crickets, pierced by the sobbing of a night-bird or the call of the toad, and in which the slightest rustle of the branches was perceptible.

We halted in the middle of the avenue to listen to the silence. Marie said in a low voice: 'I thought I heard the pine needles crackle; isn't that someone walking?' It must have been the wind, or a weasel; so many creatures devour one another, or mate, in the darkness.

'And isn't that what we are doing ourselves? And yet we're different.'

That night we came nearer than at any other moment in our lives to the truth of which both of us already had a kind of foreknowledge (I know, because we spoke about it for a long time, barefoot on the balcony, at the time when silence was deepest); that human love is the prefiguration of that love which created us – but that sometimes, as happened between us two that night, guilty though our love might be it resembled the love between the creator and his creature, and that the happiness with which we were overflowing, Marie and I, was as it were a sign of pardon granted beforehand.

I had fallen asleep. I woke to hear a sob. I took her in my arms: why was she crying? I could not understand at first what she kept saying in a low voice: 'nevermore! nevermore!'

'Oh no, Marie; for ever and for ever.'

She protested: 'You don't know what you're saying.'

The strangest thing was that at that moment nothing endured of my suspicions. The discovery that she had induced me, not perhaps by cunning and assuredly through love, but nevertheless had induced me to make this solemn promise to bind myself to her for ever, weighed little against the revelation I had that night. There is no falsehood about the happiness two people give one another. That at least is true, and it was truer for me than for any other lad of my age, since Marie had cured me, had freed me from some nameless interdict. For a moment, perhaps? No, surely not; for ever, for ever!

'You see,' I told her, 'what I disliked about our plan, what I even loathed about it, was having to lie to my mother again, to make her believe I wanted to marry you. And now, my darling, I shall look her in the face and tell her: I want you to meet my fiancée . . . And it will be true. Are you crying? Why are you crying?'

'Your fiancée . . . You're right; that will have been true at least. I shall have been your fiancée "for real", as children say.'

I asked her if that night she had not been my wife 'for real'. 'Yes, tonight . . . There'll have been tonight.'

I said: 'And every other night of both our lives . . .' The cocks calling from farm to farm heralded dawn. Prudent's wife would soon be up. Before returning to her room, Marie went back with me on to the balcony, in spite of the mist which the pine branches seemed trying to fling off. She sighed:

'Maltaverne, I'm looking at you, I'm looking at you, as though I were ever likely to forget you . . .'

I said: 'Someone's walking in the avenue.' We went back into the bedroom. It must have been Prudent or his wife. The mist, in any case, made us invisible, and we had been speaking low. Our last embrace was brief. She returned to her own room and I slid deliciously into sleep, from which Prudent's wife aroused me, bringing the breakfast tray. She had already taken the lady her coffee. I asked her whether it was herself or her husband whom I had heard walking outside the house about six o'clock. No, it was neither of them. I must have been . . . She hesitated. Madame had given leave to Jeannette Séris to play in the park when Monsieur was away. She spent her whole time there, as if she were at home. She had probably

come early this morning to take up the nets she had laid last night in
the Hure.

'She was there last night?'

'Oh, she must have kept well out of sight, and made no noise.'

I dressed hurriedly, and we all three met in the Dubercs' kitchen
to discuss the situation. It seemed certain that Mother must have
commissioned the Louse to spy on us and that as soon as she came
home she would learn everything. We had no alternative. I decided
to leave for Bordeaux with the others and to entrust Prudent with
the letter which would tell my mother about my engagement.
Simon would stay with me in the Rue de Cheverus; he could sleep
in Laurent's bed. It's true that Bordeaux in August is uninhabitable,
but 'our house in the Rue de Cheverus is a real ice-box', according
to Mother. If things took place as we had foreseen, as soon as my
mother and the Dubercs had left Maltaverne we would settle down
there for good.

Of the three of us, Simon seemed the one most excited by the
opening of hostilities. He must have been aware of what that night
had been for Marie and myself, but it did not seem to distress him.

We spent the morning in the Dubercs' kitchen, weighing every
word of the letter which was to deal the first blow to my mother,
and which Prudent was to hand to her as soon as she got out of the
car. There was a first version, entirely my own, eloquent and angry,
in which I poured forth all my rancour, and which pleased Simon
but not Marie; I yielded to her arguments. We settled on a brief,
irreproachable letter: 'In your absence, I have been visited here by a
young woman to whom I am engaged and whom I am anxious to
introduce to you. We have known one another for several months.
She works at Bard's bookshop and she is highly cultured. She had a
difficult time in her youth . . .' I spoke of the sad death of her father,

of which my mother had no doubt heard. Simon asked: 'Aren't you afraid she'll have a stroke?' I sensed that he himself was shocked by this engagement (even though he assumed it to be imaginary). A shop-assistant from Bard's to marry the Gajac son and heir! It was so incredible that Madame would not believe it, but would suspect the trap.

We had to make sure that Prudent would not betray us. He had always been ambitious for his brother. And now Simon was coming back to Maltaverne, and all his diplomas would be less than useless! Prudent, although he was the elder, could not hope to take his father's place, since, while he could count, he could neither read nor write; but Simon's return must have spelt failure to him.

While the two brothers were arguing in the kitchen, Marie said she would like to go and watch the waters of the Hure which she had heard flowing in the night. But the Louse would be spying on us, might perhaps follow us, hiding behind the pine trees. I could not endure the thought of finding myself face to face with that hideous child. 'I'd be capable of strangling her!'

Marie asked me whether we could reach the Hure without going through the park. Yes, indeed, there were plenty of sandy tracks where there was no danger of the Louse being on the watch. We went out. A little coolness still lingered with trails of mist, but we soon heard a cicada, then two, then three, answering one another discordantly. I said to Marie: 'Don't think I shall oblige you to live in this inhuman climate. We'll come back to rediscover the place at certain seasons . . .' She did not answer me. She was trudging wearily through the sand. The writing of that letter must have been horribly painful to her. She said: 'Whatever your mother is going to feel when she reads it, well, she'll be quite justified in feeling it. She doesn't know that I'm ten years older than you are . . . what I have been during those ten years . . . and what you are yourself . . .'

'What I am? What virtue is there in having gone on so long

being a child, till I became that monster that you called an angel? And as for you, Marie, those that should have been your guardians were ravening wolves . . .'

I saw that she was weeping. We were in a meadow, on the bank of the Hure. We sat down on a fallen alder. She leaned against me, still weeping. I said: 'Take care of the nettles.' The nettles all round us would be changed in my memory to mint, whose fragrant leaves I should rub between my fingers; and that meagre stream, flowing under the alders, a number of which had been felled, would be linked as it had always been with grief over the endless passing of things; it carried me away like everything else and I counted no more than the scraps of pine-bark, carved into boats, that Laurent and I used to sail on it. And the woman clinging to me, who had stopped weeping, that poor body that others had made use of, which I had chosen to take under my care for the rest of my life . . .

The mist did not disperse, but such sunlight as filtered through it was oppressive. There was thunder in the air. Perhaps it would rain at last over that parched *lande* where fires started up every day, lit by shepherds, it was said, but actually no more was needed than a ray of sunlight on a broken bottle . . . What a strange alchemy was at work within me, transfiguring all these insignificant things – as though having happened gave them a title to transfiguration!

It was better to wait in the cool of the Dubercs' house till the time came to take the train at Nizan station, ten kilometres from Maltaverne. We were to drive there in Prudent's cart. I warned Marie that we should have to set off, after a hasty lunch, at that time of day when the heat is so great that not even the animals venture outside. Marie murmured: 'Not even the Louse!'

Under the two o'clock sunshine, that journey in the cart, amid a cloud of buzzing flies, along a dusty, rutted road, was the nightmare end of our midsummer night's dream. I was sitting on the back seat beside Simon, who was sweating. I had put my hand behind Marie's back to deaden the jolts. She sat silent and rigid, and with that peculiar faculty I have for sensing what another person refrains from expressing, I knew that within her the enchanted Maltaverne of last night had turned into an accursed land from which we must escape without a backward look. We heard a motor horn, then the noise of a car. Stella, the old mare, shied; we were passed by a Serpollet driven by a monster in goggles. The dust enveloped us to such a point that Prudent had to halt for a moment at the side of the road.

The train was late. We waited, almost alone, on the sunbaked platform of that deserted station, surrounded by cages in which hens were dying of thirst.

IX

Marie begged me not to visit her in the Rue de l'Eglise Saint-Seurin while her mother was away at Soulac. We could meet at leisure in her den at the bookshop. In the Rue de Cheverus, our staircase seemed deliciously cool after the street. During the three days that Simon and I lived there together, waiting for an answer from 'Madame', we often left the little drawing-room and went to sit on the steps of that ice-cold stairway.

The nights, worse than the days, brought out the innumerable army of the largest, most venomous mosquitoes that ever existed in our latitudes. As I had a mosquito net, I merely had to make sure, before falling asleep, that no ferocious creature was shut up with me in my cage, but Laurent's bed no longer had such protection. I saw next morning that Simon was disfigured by a bite on his eyelid. He showed surprise at my concern.

'It's nothing, Monsieur Alain. My goodness, if one had to worry about mosquitoes, about a little swelling on one's eye!'

He had managed to sleep none the less, and had gone out at dawn. Had he been to Mass? I dared not ask him, but I felt sure of it. After lunch we met again in the cool gloom of the bookshop, where customers were sparse. Bard was staying at Arcachon and had left everything to Marie. Balège was ill, or pretending to be. Among the new works displayed in the window I found an anthology of modern poetry edited by Léautaud and Van Bever, and discovered one treasure after another. There was, in particular, one poem by Francis Jammes: *Il va neiger dans quelques jours . . .* which enchanted me, making my heart ache with joy, but I could not share my delight either with Marie, who was insensitive to this sort of poetry, nor with Simon, who was insensitive to any sort of poetry, and who was waiting, with greater anguish than either of us, for an answer from 'Madame'. He urged me to go back: 'It'll soon be time for the mail.'

We crossed the Rue Sainte-Catherine and took the narrow Rue Margaux towards the Rue de Cheverus. I walked a little way behind Simon, my mind full of some fantasy, staring at the pavement. Suddenly Simon's cry rang out in my ear, although he had tried to muffle it:

'Madame's there! Madame is back!'

I looked up in alarm. Yes, the De Dion, that familiar monster, was drawn up in front of the door. What were we to do? I advised Simon to go back to the bookshop and warn Marie. I would face my mother by myself, and as soon as possible I would join them. He needed no pressing to make his escape. I was coward enough to envy him, as I went forward alone to brave the wrathful and dreaded deity. How had we been foolish enough to assume that she could only answer by letter, and not to foresee that she would appear in flesh and blood and sweep down on us?

In fact this had not been her first reaction, three days had passed since Prudent had handed her our letter. I soon learned what had decided her to come and hunt me out in the Rue de Cheverus. As soon as I entered the little drawing-room, where she was standing, her hat still on her head, she drew me to her:

'My poor boy. Fortunately I'm not too late!'

She was convinced that on hearing what she had to tell me I would no longer be able to think of that creature without repulsion. I learned that our letter had left her stunned for two whole days. Then she had been to the presbytery to ask the Doyen for his advice, and what she had learnt there was even more horrifying than the shocking story of the tax-collector. When the scandal broke out,

M. le Doyen had been assistant priest at Lesparre. During the summer he had intermittent but fairly close relations with Father X . . . So he had been kept informed of another scandal which was never revealed, but which was infinitely more dreadful than the first.

In my mother's eyes a woman capable of seducing a priest, a member of a religious order, of sinning with him or even, she corrected herself, of attempting to do so (for supposing nothing had actually happened, as the friends of Father X . . . maintained, one must not commit the sin of hasty judgment), such a woman must be possessed by the devil, an accursed creature, and mere contact with her must transmit the curse, like a shameful and incurable disease.

'You see, it has left you speechless with disgust!'

'Why no, Maman dear, I knew.'

'You knew!'

Stupefaction silenced her. I knew, and yet I was willing to give my name to such a creature, to introduce her to my mother, to hand over Maltaverne to her, bind myself to her for ever? She hid her face in her hands, a theatrical gesture that was familiar to me: 'My God,' she moaned, 'what have I done to You?' As usual, the gesture was accompanied by a complaint against God.

'Try to understand, Maman.'

I reminded her that the same event looked different seen from different angles. All the members of Father X . . .'s Order had united in his defence, imputing all the blame to a bad woman, a neurotic girl who had sought to ruin him but had failed. This was the warning bell that had alarmed our curé. But in fact the girl in the case had been very young, very devout, a fervent disciple of Father X . . ., having recently suffered an appalling blow and with no one else to turn to in her distress.

'I know what she went through over that business and its horrible sequel, which you have never heard: it was an absolute martyrdom

for the child she was. And now,' I added, 'she is the woman I have
been fortunate enough to meet.'

'You've gone crazy, my poor boy, she's made you crazy!'

This was not the wrathful deity we had expected but a heartbroken
mother, an afflicted Christian, strengthened rather than shaken in
her convictions by what I had just said. In any case I have never
known Mother yield to arguments or even appear to have listened
to them. She hunted in her bag for her handkerchief, standing there
in the middle of the room, staring at the monster I had become. She
blew her nose, wiped her eyes. I tried to draw her to me to kiss her,
but she broke away as if she dreaded contact with me. Perhaps she
really was afraid of it?

'Listen, Alain . . .'

It was obvious that I was bewitched, possessed, that she would get
nothing out of me, but surely the least concession I could make my
mother was to take time to think things over; considering my age,
such a delay would have been necessary even in the case of a normal
engagement to a girl of our own social class. Mother spoke without
raising her voice; she felt on solid ground. Nobody, surely, could
have thought her suggestion unreasonable. I made a vague gesture
of acquiescence.

'Let's say a year . . . In a year's time we'll discuss it again.'

I felt the noose round my neck. I fought back: I would concede
only the four months till New Year's Day. Four months, after all,
provided a breathing-space; we'd wait and see. She asked me to
promise to devote the time to her, not to leave her side before
Christmas.

'Unless,' I said at a venture, 'next term my work should require
me to go to Paris.'

'What work?'

'My thesis.'

'A thesis? You? What thesis?'

'But I've told you about it. You never listen when I tell you about my work. It's on the origins of the Franciscan movement in France. My professor, Albert Dufourcq, suggested it to me.'

She had stopped listening already. She took off her hat, slowly pulling out the long hatpins. I asked her whether she was going back to Maltaverne. No, she had no intention of leaving me on my own. She had wired to Louis Larpe and his wife. They were coming that evening.

'And then we'll go wherever you like, or we can stay in Bordeaux. I'm at your orders, as in fact I have always been.'

What was to be done? God, how could I have been childish enough to believe (though after all the three of us had believed it) that reality would necessarily conform to a plan made by us, that everything would happen as we had determined, that my mother would react as we had decided she should?

'I have something else to ask you, Alain, and this you won't refuse me: to be willing to see M. le Doyen. He's coming to lunch to-morrow. You can speak to him or not, as you choose.'

While my mother was in her bedroom I went into Laurent's, and hurriedly packed Simon's suitcase; I took the sheets off the bed and hid them under the chest of drawers. Sweating and exhausted, I lugged the case to the bookshop. Marie was busy selling a Baedeker Guide to South-west France; when she joined Simon and me in her den, he was showering questions on me: 'Oh, my poor Simon,' I had told him, 'I can assure you it's not a case of "*Madame se meurt, madame est morte*".'

I gave them as faithful an account as I could of what had happened between Mother and myself. 'She got the better of me, as she always has done, as she always will, to the end of her days . . .' Marie protested:

'But my dear boy, you could be completely master of the situation if you wanted to. There's nothing your mother won't agree to, in order to get the engagement broken off . . . at any rate nothing in the immediate future, for make no mistake about it, the one thing she'll never give up is the Séris estate, that vast empire of pine-trees and sand over which she hopes to reign before she dies, that furnace . . .'

'But Marie,' I protested in a whisper, 'we're engaged "for real".'

She shook her head, and as Simon had gone into the shop so as to leave us alone together, she said to me: 'Yes, you'll have believed that, at least for a few minutes of that night of ours. Bless you for those few minutes. But you know in your heart it wasn't "for real".'

'Why, Marie, why?'

The relief I felt appalled me. Simon joined us without seeing us, absorbed in his reflections.

'We've been idiots,' he said. 'I thought at first that Prudent had betrayed us. No, Madame must actually have intended, for a few days, to blackmail you by deserting Maltaverne and taking my father with her. But she knows that even in our village there'd be more candidates for Father's place than you could interview in a day. As for his knowledge of the boundaries, it's useful of course, but not indispensable; there's the ordnance survey . . .'

'And then it's possible,' I said to Marie, 'that when my mother found out from M. le Doyen who you were and what you'd made of Bard's bookshop she realized what you'd be able to do with Maltaverne. Between ourselves, my mother scarcely deserves her reputation as a business woman. Her physical passion for her estate takes the form of pride in the number of pine trees she has standing, whereas many of them which ought to be cut down are rotting and losing their value. If you were mistress of Maltaverne you'd be able to make hundreds of thousands of francs out of it without damage to the property, in fact the reverse . . .'

She asked me, laughing, if I was trying to tempt her or to tantalize her. And when I protested:

'Oh,' she sighed, 'you're your mother's son all right!' (and in a whisper) 'you're really as obstinate as she is.'

'Yes,' I muttered, hanging my head. 'D'you know what's obsessing me? I know what I shall be like in 1970. I've often told you of the old man of Lassus . . .'

Marie left me to serve a customer, but Simon had heard me.

'What about me, Monsieur Alain? What shall I be like in 1970? or rather, what shall I have been like, for there'll be nothing left of me by then but a few bones. I shall have been nothing, while *you* will have lived, I don't know what sort of life, but you'll have had a life-story that can be told, that you'll be able to tell yourself, since I, your witness, won't be there. You'll still win the first prize for composition in 1970, you'll see! But as for me . . .'

'As for you, Simon, we know now that you're back at your starting-point. The kingdom you thought you had deserted was within you, and wherever you are, there it will be.'

'Never!' he protested with that muffled violence that his accent made so grotesque. 'Hey, if you think I'm going to beg them to take me back!'

I did not answer, but after a pause, when I saw that he had calmed down, I asked him casually if he still saw M. le Doyen sometimes. No, he said; but they wrote to one another from time to time; '*he's* not dropped me.'

'He's lunching with us tomorrow, Rue de Cheverus. Shall I suggest we call in at the bookshop at about this time?'

Simon uttered no further protest; a slight flush coloured his stony cheeks, as on that first occasion when he recognized me in the Rue Sainte-Catherine. He said: 'I'll be glad to see him again . . . but as a friend, not as a director. That's all over and done with. I need no one's help to know what I have to do.'

'No one's, Simon, except his, perhaps. There is always somebody, for good or evil, who sees more clearly into ourselves than we can do, who can interpret us better. For me there was Donzac, then Marie, and there was yourself, too.'

'Me, Monsieur Alain? Me? What can I have done for you?'

'You are transparent, you've helped me to believe in Grace; you, lacking all those things that I have in overpowering abundance, so that I shall sink under the burden of my great possessions, whereas you . . .'

Donzac will realize that I am here giving form to the substance of our talks in the backroom of the bookshop, where between Simon and myself there took place an unforgettable exchange: each of us saw clearly, and defined, the other's vocation. It was not from that moment that I thought of writing; I have been writing all my life; but from that moment onward I envisaged trying to become a writer, even if it were at my own expense. What I am writing here and now might some day be published. As for the closing chapter, I'd only have to paraphrase that of *L'Education sentimentale*: 'He did not travel, he never experienced the melancholy of steamboats, chilly awakenings under canvas, the bewilderment of landscapes and ruins, the bitterness of interrupted sympathies. He did not come back, because he had never left . . .'

When I reached the far end of the Galleries I found that a violent rainstorm was flooding the fortunate city. I waited for the downpour to subside, together with other people who were expressing satisfaction and delight. But the sense of release that I felt was not due solely to that summer storm. I would come back here tomorrow, for we had arranged to meet. But I had done with the bookshop, I had left it behind me for good. The purpose for which I had entered it one day was almost fulfilled. I was breaking free from Maltaverne and my interminable childhood, and I could see ahead, at a single glance, the life I was going to live, as Simon had prophesied with such conviction; and now I was no less convinced than he, I was certain of it, I knew I was not going to die, although all round me, every day, the disease that had killed my brother Laurent was consuming so many boys and girls, and I myself had that faint patch on my left lung; no, I was not going to die, I was going to live, I was going to start living.

When the rain had stopped and I was able to cross the Rue Sainte-Catherine and make my way along the Rue Margaux to the Rue de Cheverus, I knew that I should never be able to retire to Maltaverne with Simon, but that I had to go to Paris, so that all that had to happen to me should happen, people and things each at the appointed time. And yet I should lose nothing of that Maltaverne from which I was breaking free, I should take it with me, it would be my treasure, like that which Laurent and I had buried at the foot of a pine tree to find again next holidays: just a box with a few glass marbles in it . . .

Donzac will quite rightly refuse to believe that it could all have appeared to me so clearly when I left the bookshop, and while the rainstorm was flooding the Rue Sainte-Catherine; but the elements of the vision were within me, and as I write I can still feel the joyful sensation of crossing a threshold, of beginning something. Joy! tears of joy! An endless voyage where even the storms would really bring delight. I am twenty-two years old. I am twenty-two. That's nothing to rejoice at, for it's surely terrible enough to have finished being fifteen, being eighteen. I know that every year henceforward will be a downward step that I must take . . . But I'm stopping on this rung of the ladder, my twenty-second year, or at least I'm giving myself the illusion of stopping on it, since in fact neither time nor the river Hure ever stops flowing . . .

X

Mother was waiting for me on the landing, but not anxious nor distressed as I had imagined her. She stood before me pale with fury, as I had expected to find her when she first arrived and as she had not been then. What, in heaven's name, had happened in my absence to drive her beside herself with rage?

'She's slept here! You've dared bring her to sleep here, and in your poor brother's bed! That hussy!'

How could I have failed to foresee that as soon as my back was turned the hunt would be up, and that her keen scent would take her straight to the bundle of sheets inadequately concealed under a chest of drawers?

'Dirty sheets, and I'll say they're dirty! You've slept in them too. In your mother's house, in your brother's bed. I'd never have imagined you capable of such shameful behaviour. And you dare laugh, wretched boy! What has she done to you?'

'I am not laughing, I'm just smiling sadly to see you commit your old sin of rash judgment. The young woman whom you're insulting without knowing her has never been here. And let me tell you that if she had come' (I hesitated for a moment) 'we'd have had no need of Laurent's bed.'

She did not react. She could not have understood.

'Then who has slept in that room, in those sheets? Whom did you pick up in the streets?'

'Somebody you know, Maman, somebody you've known ever since he was born.'

133

She thought I was making fun of her. When I uttered the name of Simon Duberc she was speechless for a few moments.

'Oh, that's the last straw! That renegade!'

'Loss of faith does not make a renegade. A seminarist who leaves his seminary is merely misguided.'

'He's gone over to the enemy, you know that.'

'And what if I told you that on the two days he stayed here he went to six o'clock Mass each morning?'

In fact I had no absolute proof of this. He might have gone out at dawn from an old country habit. But I could not resist the pleasure of disconcerting my poor mother, for whom at this point I felt quite sorry. I told her that she should be glad and not grieved at what she had learnt from me.

'While you were investigating the traces of my crimes, I was actually meeting Simon by arrangement and persuading him to see M. le Doyen. Not here, don't worry.'

Louis Larpe, in his white summer coat, opened the door and announced: 'Madame is served.'

I cannot remember ever seeing my mother so much at a loss as during that meal, shaken in her convictions, in that basic conviction that she was in the right about everything and, primarily, that people really were as they appeared to her and that they could not be different. If I had not deceived her, if young Duberc went to Mass every morning, she had misjudged him. It was easy enough for her to dismiss everything I had told her about 'that hussy', abiding by the cliché of the innocent boy bewitched by a bad woman; but that woman would remain for ever a mystery to her. And now Simon had reappeared. In fact he had never wholly left the scene, he had remained as a subject of dispute between Mother and M. le Doyen.

All these observations about Mother are my own imagining and correspond to a certain idea that I have of her. But then, ever since I began this journal, what I have been trying to offer Donzac if not an imaginary picture of Maltaverne, as unreal as Beauty and the Beast or Riquet with the Tuft? What really happened? My mother, whose appetite is invariably good, who always pays close attention to what is served her and of whose final judgment the cook stands in awe, touched nothing that evening and retired to her own room the minute the meal was over, leaving me free to go out. But I did not go out, and since I wished to lose nothing of the night air, which was fresh after the rain, I opened all the windows; and this obliged me, on account of the mosquitoes, to sit in darkness without reading.

Reading is so much my whole life (I sometimes wonder if it has replaced living for me) that perhaps, at twenty-two, I should not have known what lies behind that cliché 'the inner life' if I had not frequently been condemned by the mosquitoes of my native city to sit motionless in front of that shimmering piece of sky above the roofs, framed by my window. Perhaps I might never have known what I know, and which is so unbelievable that I never speak of it to anyone because I'd be dismissed as presumptuous, or idiotic, or crazy: that the words 'the Kingdom of God is within you' are true, literally, that we only have to go deep down into ourselves to find it.

If the experience I had of this that evening marks a date in my life, it was because I reached that kingdom then, as I had never reached it before, although I knew for certain that I was in a state of sin. Now I had been brought up in the belief that mortal sin cuts one off from God absolutely; which incites the sinner to abandon hope, to say 'all is lost', to give up the struggle. That evening, hearing a call I knew well and overwhelmed by a sense of guilt, I had recourse to Donzac's subterfuge, which consists in saying to oneself: 'If I were one of those countless fervent Christians who are debarred from confession because they are Calvinists or Lutherans, I should ask forgiveness directly from Him who is within me. Perfect contrition is not inaccessible, as we are taught, nor reserved exclusively for the saints; it is within our reach, as is the Kingdom of God, and it is the sesame which infallibly opens the door of that kingdom.'

I thus began by thinking about all that had happened between Marie and myself and I found that I could feel no regret for it, that I was conscious of my sin not as an offence but as a grace, and that the worst thing that could have happened to me would have been for no woman to play a part in my life . . . And yet in that case this very absence would have seemed a grace. And here my dialogue with myself was silenced. A sense of great calm pervaded me. I hummed to myself, at intervals, to Mendelssohn's music which we had learnt at school, or to Gounod's which M. le Doyen preferred, that hymn of Racine's:

> *D'un cœur qui t'aime*
> *Mon Dieu, qui peut troubler la paix?*
> *Il cherche en tout ta volonté suprême*
> *Et ne se cherche jamais.*
> *Sur la terre, dans le ciel même*
> *Est-il d'autre bonheur que la tranquille paix*
> *D'un cœur qui t'aime? .* ★

Next morning Mother did not get up. Her shutters remained closed. Her headaches were unlike anything experienced by other women; she would lie in the dark with soothing compresses on her

★ 'My God, who can disturb the peace
    Of a heart that loves Thee?
  It seeks in everything Thy sovereign will
    And never itself.
  On earth, even in heaven, is there greater happiness
    Than the tranquil peace
  Of a heart that loves Thee?'

forehead. She sent word to me to apologize to M. le Doyen for her absence. Perhaps she exaggerated her indisposition so as to make possible this tête-à-tête, which was her last hope. The Doyen found it hard to disguise the joy he felt at having a meal alone with me. An innocent and childish delight lit up his habitually careworn and sombre face, whose limp cheeks he still pulled as though he were kneading bread. He had greatly aged, and needed no barber now to tonsure him; above all he had lost his upright, self-confident walk; it was chiefly this that made him different from the priest I had known as a child.

From the very first move he made to obey 'Madame's' instructions and make me talk, I evaded him. I declared that my mother was imagining things, that the only woman who played a terribly important part in my life was herself and that my sole problem was to free myself from her, even at the cost of a marriage which was absurd in the eyes of the world. I was careful not to reassure M. le Doyen, only giving him the impression that nothing was as yet decided in my mind.

'But,' I told him, 'I'm not the person you should be interested in;' and as he protested, 'I mean that at this moment it's not me that you should be trying to save but Simon, whom I see every day. Yes, the time has come to pull him ashore; but this time he'll go of his own accord in the direction he feels impelled to, and you will only be there to make his access easier. Only be careful, remember that you have only to speak of "directing" him and you'll frighten him off.'

He listened with a humble attentiveness that touched me. The poor Doyen lavished all his unused, passionate fatherly feelings on this peasant boy, who was not heartless indeed but hardened and embittered, and of whom he talked untiringly: 'I never lost sight of him, you know, I've always watched over him from afar without his suspecting, He had pneumonia his first winter in Paris. I got in touch with his landlady and paid her something to send me a report on his health, secretly of course! Simon would have thought himself at death's door if he'd seen me prowling round his sickbed.'

Since my mother had stayed in bed, there was no reason why the Doyen should not meet Simon in the Rue de Cheverus rather than in the bookshop. He agreed, 'but we must have Madame's permission.' When I presented our request through her half-open door, Mother interrupted me in her coldest tone: 'Anything you like, provided I don't have to meet him.'

The interview took place in the little drawing-room and lasted almost two hours; then Simon slipped off without saying good-bye to me. It had been agreed between them that he would spend one more year at Talence, where the parish priest, 'that holy man the Abbé Moureau', who was a friend of the Doyen's, would look after Simon and would prepare him to return, not indeed to the Bordeaux seminary but possibly to the one at Issy-les-Moulineaux. It all needed a great deal of thought and careful preparation.

I, for my part, promised the Doyen that he would soon see me again at Maltaverne: my mother had finally succeeded in making me, reluctantly, agree to leave Bordeaux. I pretended that I had first to work in the municipal library, to make some notes which were indispensable for my thesis; but I doubt whether any one could have boasted of having seen me there throughout the whole period . . .

Now, two months later, I have opened my notebook again. What I have lived through could never be expressed in any words; there's a sort of shame which is untranslatable. What I shall be able to tell of it here will be, like all the rest, an arrangement, a stylization. But I shall try; I've got to keep my promise to Donzac . . . Actually, why do I need to give myself such a pretext? As if I did not find pleasure in reliving that shame hour by hour to the end of the story, or rather of that chapter of my story which is only just beginning?

I am writing this on October 20 with my notebook on my knees, in our pigeon-shooting hut at the place they call La Chicane, miles away from the nearest farm, on a soft misty day, a day which ought to be full of flying birds; but the woodpigeons won't fly; it's a warm day and they linger in the oak trees, stuffing themselves with acorns. I see Prudent's profile with its pointed nose and long chin as he stares up between the tree-tops at those avenues of sky along which the birds will fly, if they do fly. A farmer, after giving a whistle, joins Prudent:

'Passat palombes?'

'Nade! Nade!'

Like the Hure, the few enormous, low oaks that shelter our hut have always brought eternity home to me, have always made me acutely aware of the ephemeral character of man's condition. One wouldn't mind being a thinking reed; but a thinking insect who during the few moments it has to live finds time to mate, that's something dreadful. I shall try to set down those fragments of my experience that are not inexpressible.

If I spent so little time in the municipal library, it was not because I went almost every evening to the Rue de l'Eglise Saint-Seurin. Since I only met Marie after the bookshop closed, I could easily have fulfilled the requirements of my thesis as well as those of my passion. But during those slow, heavy hours in a city drugged by summer heat, I was incapable of doing more than waiting . . . Well, what's so sensational about that? It's what happens to everyone at a certain age, at certain moments of their life. But one has to be a Christian, as I am, or to have been one, like Marie, to believe that yielding to the instinct that ensures the propagation of living species is a matter of vital importance. Or rather one has to be one of those intransigent Christians like myself who may grant themselves leave to do something, but seek no excuse; who, if they fall, do so with their eyes open.

I was now convinced that Marie had been sincere on that day when she had revealed her distress at cutting me off from God and when I had thought she was playing a part. She had renounced God for herself, but not for me. She used to say that the elements in my character that come from Christ are inseparably blended with those that come from Cybele . . . But according to her, the Christian part prevailed: 'I don't want to spoil you,' she would say. I would protest, reminding her of our night at Maltaverne. Why had things changed, we asked ourselves? Why, almost every evening, did I creep back to the Rue de l'Eglise Saint-Seurin, after we had decided the night before that it would be the last time? Why did these relapses bear so little resemblance to our midsummer night's dream, when all the happiness in the world had been revealed to me in one instant – as if our two souls had been allowed that evening, and that evening only, to unite at the same time as our two bodies? Once again, I was condemned to feel revulsion. Who had taught me revulsion?

'What a far-fetched notion,' as my poor mother might have said. Marie was like no other woman, perhaps, because she had been a pious girl. This was no falsehood either; her suffering was infinitely greater than my own. It aged her, or at least made her seem her age, whereas according to her I still looked like an angel – whose wings were not even ruffled, she would add with mingled mockery and grief.

At home in the Rue de Cheverus Mother would be waiting for me, wandering from one room to another with that set, tragic mask she wore at moments of crisis. I made the excuse of reading in the library last as long as I could. She demanded to know, at any rate, the date when we could leave. I refused to fix one. After a week she stopped asking questions, and gave up any pretence at being taken in. She knew where I came from every evening, and that I knew she knew. She would embrace me lengthily, in order to pick up some telltale scent; but she failed to recognize something that would have delighted her: she assumed that I was caught in the spider's web, and so I was indeed, or rather my body was during the hours I spent waiting and then for the space of a few moments. She had no inkling that there was no longer any question of a permanent union between Marie and myself: from my bondage in the immediate present she deduced my eternal subjection.

I would go out in the evening, after dinner, weary and satiated. Mother knew it was for no immoral purpose, for I always asked her to accompany me. She would refuse, but her mind was at ease. Sometimes I came back after an hour, at other times later if I had been to hear the music being played under the Quincunxes during the summer months; but most frequently I merely went to the Café de la Comédie for a coffee ice or, in spite of the mosquitoes, wandered about on the terrace of the public gardens, far from the crowd that stayed listening to the band of the 57th Regiment.

Now, late in August, I felt sure of meeting nobody. But that evening there was a young man smoking a pipe on the bench where I sat, at the far end of the terrace. I settled down as far from him as possible and did not look at him. He asked me teasingly: 'What are you doing in Bordeaux in August? Why aren't you at Arcachon, or Pontaillac, or Luchon?'

I recognized a student named Keller, one of those Christians who 'go to the people', the sort of person whom I horrify without even speaking a word.

'It's presumably because I've something better to do here,' I said with a meaningful air.

He muttered: 'It doesn't surprise me.' When we had known one another at the University two years before, he had at first been attracted by me, and then had tried to preach to me; but at that period Barrès's *Sous l'Oeil des Barbares* had seemed the answer to everything, providing me with formulae with which to defend myself against the wounding mockery of my fellow-students. I used to present 'a smooth surface' to their attacks. I had taken this line with Keller, who had soon come to consider me as that most contemptible of beings, a rich self-satisfied bourgeois.

'What d'you know about me?' I retorted. 'Only what I showed you in order to get rid of you, which happened quickly enough. I could just as easily have played the noble soul, the sort of thing you like.'

'And what do all these masks conceal? Nothing very pretty, I'm sure.'

'I'm not asking you to look!'

This was said in a tone which presumably disturbed my Christian friend, for he promptly added: 'Forgive me, I realize that I had no right to take such a superior attitude. We're all of us poor creatures.'

'Yes, Keller, but there's quite a distance between a poor creature like myself, spoilt and blasé, who suffers only on his own account, and a poor creature like yourself, who hungers and thirsts after righteousness.'

'Oh, but you know, I like to enjoy myself too, after all . . . We ought to get together some time,' he added with sudden eagerness. 'I won't preach at you.'

I was feeling the need to confide in someone. The thing was choking me. I said to him: 'All right, but I'm going through a bad time. I feel terribly outcast from God.'

He took my hand and held it for a moment. 'You know what it says in the *Imitation*: "When you think you are furthest from Me, then I am closest to you."'

'But it's not only a question of coldness or aridity. I have been committing a sin.'

'Committing a sin?'

'Yes, and the person with whom I have been sinning is as anxious as I am that we should give it up . . . But there comes a moment, every day, when neither she nor I can help ourselves . . .'

'Yes, I see,' said Keller, in a tone of great earnestness. 'Well, I shall pray for you, and get others to pray. I know the Prioress of the Visitation very well.'

'Oh no,' I protested. 'It's not worth while. It's nothing, it's less than nothing.'

'You call that less than nothing?'

I got up; I had resumed the tone which used to exasperate Keller in our student days: 'Yes, I'm very humble, nobody could be humbler than I am; I don't believe that any of my actions can be of the slightest importance.'

'And yet the least of those actions involves eternity. Don't you believe that?'

'Yes, I believe it . . . But not that particular action more than any other. The worst thing about me, Keller, is not my actions or even my thoughts. The worst thing about me is my indifference to that passion that obsesses you, as a Christian, and also all young militants, Socialists or Anarchists . . . The worst thing about me is my indifference to the suffering of others, my acceptance of my own privileges.'

'You're an upper-class boy, a bourgeois, and you must kill the bourgeois in yourself. You'll see, we can do it.'

'It's easy to blame the bourgeoisie. In fact I come from those Landais peasants who work their old parents to death, and when they take a little girl into their service, a *gouge* as they say in patois, if she survives, it's because one is tough at that age. . . .'

I fell silent, ashamed of having opened my heart to this high-minded, casual acquaintance. I got up: 'Good-bye. Keller. Don't follow me. Forget what I've told you. Forget me.'

'How can you think I'll forget you! Let's see one another next term. Promise me . . .'

Poor Keller! He was going to pray and suffer for me, and to make pious women pray and suffer for me too. How crazy it was! And yet there was nothing in the world that touched me more than the communion of saints, that reversibility; my irritation with him was due to his interference in my most secret concerns and my conviction of his power to affect them, to change their course. Not that I believe that what took place next day had any connection with that meeting in the Jardin des Plantes. What happened was in the order of things possible, and even inevitable: Mother was at the end of her tether from uncertainty and anguish, time was passing, she had to intervene.

Next morning, the minute I opened my eyes I knew that at the usual time I should not need to ring at Marie's house, for she would be watching for me behind the door. It was not raining, but it must have been raining elsewhere, this was a day's respite. I roamed like a stray dog along the quayside all afternoon. I went as far as the docks. The tram brought me back, standing on the platform among a crowd of dockers. I wandered some more. What I did until the appointed time is unimportant. About half-past six, Marie was not behind the door and I rang in vain. She must have been detained. I decided to walk a little longer in the neighbourhood, but I was exhausted. I immersed myself for ten minutes in the gloom of Saint-Seurin, the darkest church in the town; then I came back to Marie's house. Just then I saw her cross the street. She was breathless and pale. She pulled the key from her pocket: 'Come in quickly.' She thrust me into the parlour, where the shutters were closed.

Before even taking off her hat she said to me: 'I've just been seeing your mother.'

'Where did you see her? Did you speak to her?'

'Yes, would you believe it? I was showing a book to a customer, I felt ill at ease under the persistent stare of a lady in black, rather stout and obviously wealthy, who had just come in. I suddenly felt that this was not a customer, but somebody who was interested in me, and at that moment I saw you yourself, Alain, yes, in that tall imperious figure, like Agrippine or Athalie, I had a sudden glimpse of your angel face. I recognized your mother, just like the picture I had formed of her. She was, quite literally, devouring me with her eyes; she was tearing me into shreds. I thought I'd known what it meant to be somebody's enemy. No: being hated, really hated, is rarer than you think; I know now the look of a person who would kill you slowly and gloat over your death, if that were allowed.

'Ought I to let her go away again? What would you have done, Alain? I yielded to my first impulse, which was basically curiosity. I went up to her and asked in the most business-like tone: "What can I do for you, Madame?" She seemed nonplussed. She pretended she had only come in to have a look at the new books. "Yes," I said, "and perhaps at me, Madame?" You can imagine her expression at that moment. "You know who I am?" "I know all about you, Madame." She turned pale, she murmured: "He's talked to you about me? I'm not surprised at anything from him now." I protested: "Oh, it's not because of what he's told me about you that I know all about you, it's because you've left such a mark on him, you've made him and moulded him, he's still so much your handi-work, even when he's about to escape from you: I know all about you in so far as I know all about him." She said: "All that's just words . . ." in the voice she must have used to tell you you were talking nonsense. She muttered: "It's impossible to talk in this shop . . ." "But there's a room behind the shop, Madame. If you can

bring yourself to come in . . ." She agreed, I asked Balège to look
after sales for a minute, and I took your mother into my den.'

'Mother in your den!'

'Yes, can you believe it, in that closet. We were on top of one
another, as you always say. The first words she spoke to me did not
match her fury; she'd prepared them beforehand, in cold blood, and
I think that as she uttered them she grew calmer and more in tune
with them. She assured me that she had no intention of passing
judgment on me, and indeed that she was anxious to believe the
good you had spoken of me because it was so much in her interest
that it should be true. "But Mademoiselle, if you are the exceptional
creature he has described to me" (there was an unconscious note of
contempt in her voice) "and loving Alain as you profess to do, you
must surely agree that nothing could be more disastrous for a lad of
twenty-two, who's still only fifteen in a great many ways . . ."

'"Who was only fifteen, Madame, until he met me."

'She understood perfectly well what I was trying to tell her; she
clenched her teeth, but restrained herself and went on: "nothing
could be more disastrous than marriage with a woman who's so
much older and, forgive me if I offend you, one who, after all, has a
past . . ." "Yes," I said, "and a present, and why not a future?" I
deliberately sought to irritate her, in order to make her speak out.
She went on: "Do you think, Mademoiselle, that there's any mother
in the world who would not be appalled at the prospect of such a
marriage? I won't remind you of what makes any connection between our two families literally impossible . . ." "True, Madame . . .
and in the first place the fact that I don't belong to any family,
whereas Alain is the Gajac son and heir, the typical upper-class
boy . . ."'

I interrupted Marie angrily. 'You belittled me in front of Mother!
You wanted to show off, to dominate her, to crush her, and you
used me as a weapon.'

'Yes,' she said, 'I admit that I took a keen pleasure in settling our accounts. I revelled in being insolent. The supreme outrage that I had on the tip of my tongue was to tell her: your son has asked me to marry him, but never fear, there's no question of my consenting: it's himself that I love, not his fortune which I loathe, not his background which revolts me . . . I'd have granted her that the difference in our ages was a threat to our happiness, my own even more than yours. Yes . . . but, Alain, I'd have been playing into her hands, and relieving her of an enormous burden: she'd have regained her mastery over your life, you'd have lost the bargaining power I've provided you with; there's nothing your mother won't agree to if I should withdraw. So I had to play my cards carefully. I began by agreeing with her, I took pains to appreciate her arguments. I admitted that from a social point of view, and indeed from every point of view, I was exactly the type of wife whom the mother of such a privileged only son would not want for him . . . Except, I added, in order to protect him from a worse fate . . .'

'Oh,' I protested, 'you didn't taunt her with her passion for the land, Numa Séris, the Louse?'

'No, I taunted her with nothing, I spoke my mind freely, but not in such a way as to drive her out in a rage. I boasted that I'd already broken almost all the bonds that shackled you, but I admitted that I'd not finished setting you free; I added that I'd have no difficulty in showing you that there's nothing so very clever about watching pines grow by themselves, and then having the resin collected by your tenant-farmers and pocketing the money; instead of leaving those that should have been cut down long ago to rot and thus losing the benefit of the new saplings, I would teach you to have regular cuttings made and would thus bring you in a huge annual income of which your tenants don't get a penny . . . But we're going to change all that, I added, and we shall share with the tenant-farmers

the profit from the timber we cut. We've decided that, Alain and
I . . .'

'It's not true, you didn't tell her that lie?'

'Why yes, I gave myself that pleasure.'

I had heard that spiteful note in Marie's voice before, in brief
spurts, emitting something of the bitterness accumulated within her
during her unhappy youth, but it had taken the meeting with my
mother to break the floodgates and let loose the great wave that now
bespattered me, too. I suddenly found myself siding with my mother,
I realized it from the cry I uttered:

'No! what business is it of yours?'

'Ah!' she exclaimed angrily, 'that's as bad as Hermione's *Qui te l'a
dit?* I wonder if it's really the insult to your mother that shocks you,
if it's not rather the suggestion of sharing the price of timber with
your tenant farmers – if it's not because I pretended to snatch that
bone from you that you suddenly show your fangs. Oh, you're your
mother's son! well, off with you to comfort her!'

I stammered: 'Marie, darling . . .' I tried to draw her to me, but
she pushed me away, wild with rage.

'In any case, there's one thing you'll never be able to do, I'm
afraid, and that's to take a woman in your arms. That's something
that can't be learnt.'

I took that blow, at first, without feeling it, my hands hanging
loose. My face must have betrayed my dismay, for in a second she
sobered up. She moaned: 'Alain, *mon petit* . . .' but it was my turn
to repulse her, and I went out, slamming the street door violently
behind me.

XI

It's raining on the oak trees of La Chicane. The indeterminate
whisper enhances the loneliness of this remote *lande*. I am sheltering in the tiny sitting-room built of pinewood and covered over
with bracken so that it is indistinguishable from the hut and does not
scare the woodpigeons. It has a fireplace where Laurent used to come
and cook the larks which he had shot in Jouanhaut's field: he did not
care for pigeon-shooting, for which one has to keep motionless. For
four years now, Laurent has been lying very still, poor lad – all that
is left of him is lying still; all that's left of that young, full-blooded
creature . . . Nothing has the least importance. This knowledge is no
help against the anguish that is caused by a precise fact, a disaster that
has taken place irreparably, and which I shall have to bear during the
sixty years ahead that I expect to live, but I shall try to master that
anguish by writing in this notebook, resuming my story where I
had left it off and reliving it minute by minute up to the final blow
that fell.

So then: Marie's door closed behind me: it's over, it's really over
this time. 'Alain, *mon petit*!' That last appeal irritated me instead of
touching me. No, I'm not your 'little one'. Old as you are, you're
not quite old enough to be my mother. I ran down the Rue de
l'Eglise Saint-Seurin, hurrying towards Mother, who might perhaps be near her death. She sometimes complains of her heart,
saying: 'In our family, they die of heart trouble.' Louis Larpe,
waiting for me on the landing, informed me that Madame had
her headache and would not be coming down to dinner. I went

into her room without knocking. She was lying down, but not in the dark, as she does when things are really bad. Her bedside lamp was lighted. She was very pale, but smiled at me and seemed quite calm. I tried not to give myself away, but how could she fail to see that I was in great distress? She drew me to her and I burst into tears, just as I used to when I'd been forgiven after a stormy scene and she would say: 'that's my good boy.'

'What's wrong, my poor darling?'

'You've been hurt, I know . . .'

'Oh, so you know? Yes, hurt . . . but helped, too. What do I care what that poor girl thinks of us? The important thing is that, basically, one must grant her this, she has measured the unbridgeable distance between herself and you, so that I'm at ease now . . .'

'Did she tell you she'd given up . . .'

'Oh, not exactly, but I understood; she showed herself in a good light. She doesn't want your money, your land, your bourgeois milieu! It's she who is turning you down, you understand?' (Mother was laughing, so ludicrous did it seem to her.) 'Well, I'm sure I've no objection!'

So nothing had happened as Marie had described it. She had recreated for my benefit a scene that was half imaginary. Why? To revenge herself for her defeat? For she had been defeated, since Mother had come back reassured.

'Yes, I'm reassured. Oh, not only because of her outburst against all that we represent for her, but also, Alain darling, because I have seen her. I admit that she has very fine eyes: one can't deny her that. But she looks much older than her age: she works for her living, doesn't she?'

'Yes,' I said, 'and she has suffered a great deal.'

'Oh! that kind of suffering . . .' Prudently, Mother restrained herself. I asked, after a pause:

'Did you speak of Maltaverne?'

'No, of course not! She hadn't the impertinence, except for her diatribe against great estates and big landowners.'

'I expect she inveighed against us for not sharing the price of timber with the tenant-farmers?'

I asked this with a noncommittal air. Standing a little aside, I watched the big pale face in the lamplight; it expressed nothing but surprise.

'What are you thinking of? You can imagine how I'd have treated her if she'd dared . . . But you've not dined, my poor boy. There's some jellied chicken. Go along and don't worry about me, I'm quite happy.'

I was hungry, and I ate greedily, under Louis Larpe's approving eye. As yet, I was not suffering. Perhaps I was not going to suffer at all? I had been a child, then a morbidly sensitive adolescent, so they said, and so I believed. No one else knew what a monster of indifference I might suddenly become, not only towards others but towards myself. Why had Marie launched out so furiously against me? Why had she sought to revenge herself on me for the fact that my mother had got the better of her, as she did of her farmers, her servants, her tenants, her tradesmen, Numa Séris, and above all myself, her wretched son? Perhaps Marie had suddenly come to hate me for all that she had once adored in me: my weakness, my incurable childishness. Surely this was too far-fetched; she had wrenched herself free from that last dream of happiness which I embodied for her . . . And what of myself? Stretched out under the mosquito net, as though under a cloud, I heard the fierce creatures buzzing all round. I felt convinced that others, more dreadful, would appear before long. I kept thinking: what of myself? I clenched my teeth; no, I was not so sensitive as they all believed, but neither was I so weak.

We left for Maltaverne two days later. The previous day I had been to say good-bye to Simon. I had visited him at Talence, where we could talk freely. I had been unable to persuade him to follow me, even for a few days. It was not only because of Madame, it was chiefly of the Duports that he was frightened. He seemed to me peaceful and relaxed; the name of M. Moureau recurred constantly in his conversation. He had put himself in M. Moureau's hands. I confessed to him that Pascal's total surrender to his director was the thing that I should find most utterly impossible. Simon no longer dreaded his final year at the Lycée. It would be a time 'to collect oneself', as he said. Later he would enter the Issy seminary: 'You'll be in Paris then, we can see one another.' There was no doubt in his mind that I should be going to Paris, that I should still be blessed and burdened with all that he would never know, save through me, in me. I told him, jokingly, that he would thus conquer the world by proxy, and while I lost my soul he would be saving his. He said in a low voice: 'Both our souls.'

I did not know that he, too, had a blow in store for me. I thought him inoffensive, incapable of doing me either good or harm – surely the most harmless of creatures. We had not exchanged one word about Marie, and the silence between us was heavy with I knew not what. I had always been used to hearing Mother, shrewd and in-quisitive, saying: 'You're hiding something from me.' I had myself formed the habit of detecting what other people were hiding from me. I asked Simon, just as I was leaving him, whether he knew about Marie and myself? Yes, he had seen her the day before. I was sorry I had mentioned her name. I felt that he was going to show a peasant's tactlessness; and he did so. He said: 'It was as if she'd had a tooth

out . . .' and added, 'It's better for both of you. Because in any case
she never believed . . . You suspected her of thinking about marriage.
But for heaven's sake, with her background! She's so intelligent that
she might perhaps have brought you to that point, but she knew it
would have been hell. She's not crazy. Only if this affair had gone on
longer it might have interfered with her plans in another direction,
although old Bard isn't all that particular.'

'What has Bard to do with Marie's private life?'

'Well, of course there's nothing of that sort between them, and
there never will be; old Bard is seventy. What it amounts to is that
Marie will marry the bookshop. After all, he's become just the
accountant and she's the spirit of the place. Her bookshop means
everything to her, you know. I swear she loves it better than
Maltaverne. You should hear her talk about the nettles along the
Hure, the flies, the journey back in the cart with horseflies pestering
the old nag, the wait at Nizan station . . .'

'If anyone ought to have understood Maltaverne, that arid
anguished land with its bleeding pine trees, it was surely she.'

'Oh no, Monsieur Alain, one has to have been born there, and to
have had one's grandfathers and great-grandfathers born there.
There's only you and me . . . She's a town person, she doesn't even
live on a street, breathing freely, but in a passage . . .'

'So you believe that she and Bard . . .'

'Oh, not before the Christmas rush, but about January 15.'

'I shall have been the last treat she's allowed herself . . . It's really
horrible.'

'Why no, since nothing will happen, since nothing can happen,
it's just the way they've arranged their lives . . .'

'And after all,' I cried, 'she's used to old men!'

'That's wrong of you, Monsieur Alain, that's very wrong!'

'Old men are horrible, when they can't keep away from young
people, it makes you sick, ageing writers who dare talk about

it in their books, who've no shame . . . To think that she's given
up her life to them! Well, she'll have had me. There's always that.
When Balège retires she can treat herself to a twenty-year-old
clerk.'

'No, Monsieur Alain, she's loved you, she still loves you.'

'Well, she'll love a twenty-year-old clerk, and then they'll murder
Bard so that they can get married. Really, there's something very
Zolaesque about that backstreet bookshop.'

'Oh, Monsieur Alain, please, that's very wrong of you . . .'

'And she's got a Zola side to her, too; all that I loathe most. How
can Thérèse Raquin understand Maltaverne? She did love it, though,
you know, she loved it on the evening you arrived, and then at night,
and again at dawn before it becomes a fiery furnace, when the pines
seemed to be blessing the two of us with their outspread branches . . .
No, they were only blessing me, they only recognized me, she had
nothing to do with them.' And I suddenly burst out: 'But of course
she's just right for Bard. She's not so much younger than he is, after
all.'

'Oh, Monsieur Alain!'

'When a woman's past her first youth she's gone over to the other
side, to Bard's side.'

I had not known that pain could drive me to such fury. I shouted:
'To think of all those priests secretly bewailing their celibacy, when
they ought to be thankful for being spared such beastliness. And even
so, beasts are less revolting.'

'Oh, Monsieur Alain, you're talking nonsense, as Madame would
say. The flesh is holy, you know.'

I burst out sobbing: 'Yes, I know.' Simon had no notion what to
do or say when someone like Monsieur Alain broke into tears before
him. From a child, he had never wept in front of anyone, nor even
by himself. Tears were another of my privileges.

I quickly pulled myself together, wiped my eyes, apologized: it was only the shock of Marie's marriage to an old man. I was already getting used to the idea. After all, she was marrying the bookshop; what could be better? Everything was all right . . . I got into the car. I would see Simon when term began. In the De Dion I started suffering again. It was not what I usually called suffering. It hurt me physically, it was physically unbearable. She knew, she had always known, she had treated herself to the innocent that I was before settling down. When she became Madame Bard she would have to behave. What was this pain? It could not last. If I hadn't had to leave for Maltaverne next day I'd have got in touch with Keller, he'd have taken me to his community, Le Sillon, I might perhaps have met somebody. He had told me: 'Le Sillon means friendship.' It meant love, without beastliness.

Next day, we were at Maltaverne. I had turned down any suggestion of Luchon, or of hotel life anywhere. Mother could see that I was unhappy; it would be over in a few days, I'd recover from my operation. It was the inevitable reaction. She herself seemed more relaxed than she had been for years, pacified, like someone who has just escaped from mortal danger. Not for a moment did she suspect that she had never been closer to what would have been, for her, the greatest misfortune of all; that she had never been so close to it as during the moments of respite that are still granted me. What I am writing here is for myself alone, even Donzac shan't read it, since there is nothing more shameful, more contemptible, than to pretend to want to die and then not to die. A failed suicide is always suspect; but to be not even capable of such a failure! Better not make oneself a laughing-stock.

The fact remains that between my visit to Simon, the day before we left for Maltaverne, and today, I was only protected from that crazy urge to go to sleep for ever, that will-not-to-live, by what? I know nothing of what doctors know about this disease, but I know what it is to be a poor creature who represents one moment in his race, whose great-grandfather and great-grand-uncle drowned themselves in a pool in the Techoueyre, smitten, perhaps, by that disease that shepherds call 'pellagra', which drives its victims to drown themselves. I know that theirs is a disease like all those of which we carry the seeds within ourselves, that it exudes an anguish that can kill, that it constitutes the very centre of our being, ever since we first came into the world, and that our earliest crying told of it.

During these last weeks spent in Mother's company, whereas she was radiantly calm and indulged me in every way, going to the trouble of procuring crayfish and *cèpes* for me to eat, I can admit to myself that only my own clumsiness preserved me from death. 'You're useless with your hands,' Mother has so often taunted me, 'you'd not even be capable of doing a porter's job.' No, nor even of killing myself. The Techoueyre pool is too shallow nowadays. As for poison . . . what can one get from the chemist's without a prescription? Too cowardly to face Anna Karenina's death under a train, too cowardly to jump from a height, too cowardly to press a trigger.

The strangest part is that the one necessity for me, my faith in eternal life, hardly came into account. Behind the definitions in the catechism, behind the casuists' prohibitions, I seem to hear a mocking laugh: these idiots identify with murder the act of freely leaving the world . . . For one thing, there's no freedom about it, since we inherit the need to do it, like everything else that kills us gradually day by day, from birth till death. Since my return I no longer see Maltaverne as anything more than what it is: a bleak arid heathland, which will end as scorched earth. It was my own gaze that transfigured it, like a magicians. Marie, too: Maltaverne and Marie are now for ever as they really are. I have lost my power of transfiguring them. Above all, Marie must not believe that it's on her account that I have wished to die.

I try to pray, but the words shed all their meaning as I utter them, and that refuge beyond words to which I had so often had recourse, thinking it a state of contemplation, is now merely a gap opening on to the void, on to nothing.

Once again, there have been moments of respite. I suddenly recover my zest for life. I know it will not last, that my sickness will recur, but I take advantage of the moment granted me to get my breath again. On a fine night, I rose and went barefoot on to the balcony where Marie and I had leaned. Yes, something did exist: all that lay before my eyes once more, that sky where the stars were growing pale, the tops of the pine trees that seemed so close to it, and my eyes gazing on them, and my despairing heart. These things *were*, at any rate, and I had lied when I asserted that there was nothing, and the fact that I had no key to the absurd universe was no proof that the key did not exist.

These periods of respite grew more frequent up till the incident I am about to tell – or what I thought was just an incident, but was in fact the turning in my path where I was to be assailed, seized by the throat, as though the urge to kill myself had been the harbinger of imminent disaster. Although in September nobody bathes in M. Lapeyre's mill-pond, where the water is icy, it was so hot that day that I took my swimming trunks along with me. I probably had, at the back of my mind, the thought of ending it all that day, for it was highly probable that I should be all alone. I lacked courage, I knew, to face Anna Karenina's death, but not Ophelia's – perhaps because I knew that I should instinctively make those movements which would prevent me from sinking. I imagined Mother's grief, and Marie's. People would say what they always say: that I'd been seized with cramp or had a stroke. There would be no witness.

I hurried down the sandy path towards the mill and discovered to my annoyance that a solitary bather was splashing about in the pond. The water is so cold that you don't linger there. So I decided to wait until he had cleared off, and slid among the bracken from which, unseen, I could keep my eyes on him. There is an inadmissible pleasure, to which I now admit, in watching some one who does not see you, who does not know that you are there but believes himself to be alone; a really godlike pleasure. I soon discovered that my bather was a girl, but so slender and long-legged that the mistake was easy. No longer quite a little girl; you never know with girls, they are never children, childishness is denied them. The proof that she was a very young girl was that she wore a swimsuit like a boy's. A village girl would never have dared. She came out of the water and sat on the bank, in the sun, to dry herself, looking round her, in the noontide solitude and silence. She slipped down the top of her bathing suit, baring her shoulders and her nascent breasts. What I then experienced was not, as Donzac may think, a faun's delight. No, I've not reached the stage of lusting after little girls. I felt as if the grasp that was throttling me had loosened (if I had only known!) and it was as though a hand were laid on my blind eyes and then withdrawn, and suddenly I could see. A single being like this was a marvel, and there were millions of them in the world – that world which I did not know, and which in fact nothing and nobody could force me to explore if I preferred to stay in one room, where my books are and where other men are not.

She stood there for a long moment in the sun, the little girl, and what I felt as I watched her was something utterly innocent: it was a conviction, which is doubtless valid only for myself but which I always feel at the sight of a young comely body, that God exists. You can see, God exists. So that the same voice that shouts in my ear: 'everything is there, everything is awaiting you, kill and

eat . . .' also whispers: 'but you may choose to renounce it all and to
seek Me, and that is the only real adventure.'

The little girl had disappeared into the bracken and emerged a
minute later, in her short frock, not pretty so far as I could judge at
a distance, with her hair strained back from a high forehead and
held in place by a round comb. But I had seen her undressed and I
knew that she was beautiful, not with an immutable beauty of
feature but with that inherent in a line that must vanish, linked to a
moment of transition, I had surprised a moment between dawn and
sunrise, or rather between sunrise and morning – the wonder which
will not last is there already without really having begun.

I let her run off, and followed her at a distance. She walked on,
upright and serious, like a grown-up girl; then she would suddenly
leap like a mountain goat into the bracken, bend down to pick up
something, and then set off again. At one point a dead twig snapped
under my sandal. She turned round, raised her little hand to her eyes
to see who was coming, and all of a sudden – had she recognized me?
She darted off, disappeared round a bend in the path and when I
reached it myself she must have run into the woods, for I could no
longer see her.

XII

When I got back from the mill, my mind still engrossed with the vision of that startled bather, Mother was waiting for me on the terrace. She called out that there was a telegram for me. She held it out, open: 'I opened it, of course! It's from Simon . . . such impertinence!' I read: 'Must see you urgently. Wire if you can come Talence tomorrow.'

'My advice would be to insist on his writing to tell you what it's all about.'

'No, he's the most considerate creature; he must have some very serious motive. I shall go there tomorrow. I'll warn the chauffeur.'

'Just as you like! It's your car and your chauffeur.'

In the early morning mist the cocks of Maltaverne were answering those in distant farmyards. 'A call echoed by a thousand sentries.' I was sure the summons came from Marie and that I should find her at Simon's. I did not even feel curious about it, being resolved to avoid any arguments; when a woman is such an actress one need not pretend to believe in the reality of the part she plays, however convinced she may be, however adept at self-deception. Donzac describes Bourget's novels as 'twopenny psychology'. Yes, and it is with such small coin that we pay one another. And then, although I had reached a turning-point just then, I was too exhausted myself. I could feel nothing. I laughed to myself in the car at the thought that my bitterest resentment against Marie was due to what she had said to Simon about the nettles by the Hure, and the flies, and the cart, and Nizan station, to her repudiation of Maltaverne, the ungrateful, unworthy, idiotic creature.

She was not at Simon's when I arrived there, but she was to join us at lunch time. Bard was frantic, so Simon told me, because Marie had had to interrupt her work. She was breaking her heart because she had not been able to account to me personally for that marriage scheme, which she envisaged as a means of ensuring that the book-shop should not change hands. Simon admitted that he had given her too black a picture of my fury when he had rashly spoken to me of the scheme, assuming I already knew of it.

'You're always telling things,' I reproached him angrily. 'You make everything so much worse. Tact is a virtue that can't be learnt, unfortunately.'

He put up a poor defence. He must have had many other sins of the same sort on his conscience.

Marie arrived by tram shortly before noon. The thing that was about to overwhelm us, and of which I could have had no concep-tion at the time, now that it has happened prevents me from fixing my thoughts on the confused conversation I had with Marie when Simon left us alone together in his room. I must say to Marie's credit that as soon as she saw my unhappy face her only anxiety was on my behalf. I seem to have the gift of bringing out the anxious mother in women. She took my head between her two hands and said: 'I don't like the look in your eyes.'

I accepted without argument all the reasons she gave me for her marriage, as if it no longer concerned me. The few hours that followed Marie's explanations and our lunch at the Talence bistro to which Simon took us seem to me an almost infinite space of time, a cleft in my life between two worlds; as if the true reason for my anguish had suddenly been revealed to me, as if that banal caption under a photograph in the *Petite Gironde*, brought me this morning,

with my coffee, by the concierge of the Rue de Cheverus, had
served to send me hurtling into a bottomless abyss.

This morning then, after drinking a few sips of coffee, I cast a
casual glance at the front page of the newspaper, and I thought I was
suffering from a hallucination: the unsmiling face of the little girl
with her hair strained back over too high a forehead was one that I
recognized. It was the little girl I'd seen at the mill. And beneath it,
in italics: 'Jeannette Séris, daughter of M. Numa Séris, left her
father's home the day before yesterday in the afternoon and has not
returned. It is possible that she may have run off, as on some previous occasions. She was wearing a striped jersey and white espad-
rilles, without socks, and her hair was held with a round comb.' Then
followed the address of Numa Séris and a telephone number. It was
the Louse! Before settling down to absorb and brood over the
anguish that this story held in store for me, I dwelt for a while on the
irony of it: it was the Louse that I had seen at M. Lapeyre's mill and
had found so adorable! Someone had played a trick on me; it
could not be chance, it was too cunningly contrived. 'An enemy
hath done this . . .' Yes, it was the enemy who had made her seem
so lovely; but she herself had been terrified by the sight of me and
had disappeared, perhaps for ever.

I was the only witness. I had to get back to Maltaverne, as soon as
possible, but I had arranged to meet Marie and Simon at midday. I
would tell them everything, I would do whatever they advised me
to do. After all, it must have been a childish escapade; I had not
known she was liable to them, no one ever talked about her in my
presence. My God, why are You mocking me?

I dressed hurriedly, I went out, I bought the two other Bordeaux
papers, where I found the same photograph with the same caption;
I went into the offices of the Crédit Lyonnais and those of the newspaper *La France* in the Rue Porte-Dijeaux, where the latest news was

posted up; there was nothing there about the disappearance of the Séris child. I came back to the Rue de Cheverus. I confess that I was shaking with fear and sweating with anguish. Fear of what, anguish about what? I was sure I had to expect the worst. If that worst happened, well, this time I should find strength and means to pass over to the other side. The enemy should not get me, for all his cunning contrivances.

It was as though I held in my hands a noose which still hung slackly about my neck but was tightening second by second. At twelve o'clock I was waiting behind the door, and I opened it before they had time to ring. I don't know what I can have looked like. Marie exclaimed: 'Alain, what's the matter?' I could not speak, but showed them the photograph. Well, what of it? They had seen it, and laughed at first; it was some childish escapade. I protested: 'It's no laughing matter, I'm in it up to my neck.'

'You're crazy, Alain!'

Then I began telling them the story. I did not recognize my own voice. They had stopped laughing. Marie said: 'We'll have lunch, and then you shall go back. They'll have found her by this evening. You can make your statement as soon as you get home.' As I could not have eaten anything Marie suggested going to Prévost's for a cup of chocolate.

'You'll merely have the unpleasantness of having to make a state-ment . . .'

'And of seeing your name in all the papers,' Simon broke in.

Marie stared at him, shrugged her shoulders and suggested going to the bookshop where she could telephone to the news editor of the *Petite Gironde*, who was one of her best customers; he might be able to reassure me.

The bookshop was closed at this time of day and we went in by a private door. Marie's friend was not in his office, but she had his home number and was able to reach him quickly. She held out the receiver to me. Yes, there was fresh news: 'a resin-tapper had seen the little girl running past him as if she had been frightened or even pursued, by someone or something. The man was being closely questioned. He was still considered only as a witness, but . . .' I let the receiver drop.

'Alain, why panic?'

'The man was speaking the truth, she was running because she was frightened. It was of me she was frightened: of me, who had just been watching her bathing . . .'

'Yes, and who, a quarter of an hour later, were back at Malta-verne, where you were given Simon's telegram. What are you so afraid of?'

Simon shook his head. 'Well, for heaven's sake, if you think there's nothing to worry about . . .'

'Shut up, you fool,' she cried angrily. 'Just look at his poor face. I was going to ask you to go to Maltaverne with him; on second thoughts, he'd be better off alone than with you . . . And yet, no! I'll go with him myself. You stay here till Balège appears; explain the position, and help him out if need be. I'll be back tomorrow morning.'

'But what will Madame say when she sees you?'

'She'll see her son too, and one look will be enough. She'll under-stand, she's not like you who understand nothing.'

I had a sense of release, I committed myself into her hands, noth-ing dreadful could happen to me so long as she was there. I could breathe again. The car crawled along the crowded Rue Sainte-Catherine; then we were out on the Léognan road, and the first pine trees appeared. Marie held my hand. She asked me: 'You're not frightened any more?' No, I was not frightened any more, but I knew that my fears would revive. It was obvious to me now that I could not be suspected, but in less than ten minutes it would be so no longer. Then I should feel convinced that everything pointed to my guilt.

'Even you, Marie, if they questioned you and you told everything you know, would be a hostile witness.'

'Careful, Alain, you're giving way again . . .'

'You remember, the morning we left, when you wanted to see the Hure and I took a short cut because we knew the child was spying on us, you remember what I said about her? I told you: "I'll strangle her!"'

'You're dreaming, Alain. In any case it's of no importance.'

'All the same, if you were questioned, it would be your duty to mention that revealing remark.'

'Which reveals nothing except a momentary irritation which I felt myself, which anybody would have felt . . .'

'She must have known I detested her, since she was so afraid of me, since the mere sight of me, as she stood at that turning in the path, was enough to send her running into the wood where that man was waiting for her.'

'It's the fault of Fate, as Charles Bovary says, it's not your fault at any rate.'

'A twig snapped under my sandal, and she turned her head and saw me. I might have put my foot down beside the twig and then she'd have followed the sandy track as far as Maltaverne. And the fact that I had seen her naked at that particular moment, that I discovered at that moment that I'd been wrong about her and that she had become as different from the little girl we used to call the Louse as a butterfly is from a caterpillar . . .'

Marie murmured, after a silence: 'What a disaster for your mother!'

'So really you understand her feelings?'

Yes, she understood them. We said nothing more. She held my hand from time to time, pressing it a little to remind me of her presence: 'don't be afraid, I am here.' It was what Mother used to say when I was frightened in the night. Marie knew what was the matter with me, she'd been able to study the same symptoms in one of her old men: 'you told Simon I was used to old men . . .' Really, he repeated everything!

'Yes, he repeats everything. Well, I saw one of those old men nearly choked to death by the nightmares he invented.'

At Villandraut, where we stopped for petrol, there were people arguing in front of the garage. When the chauffeur got back to the car he told us: 'The bastard has confessed; he strangled her and hid the body in a sheepfold, and then at night he took it in a wheel-barrow to a deep hole in the Hure above the mill.' I covered my face with both hands, not to hide my tears from Marie but to shut out that world which I had not been brave enough to leave.

Mother, sitting alone in the drawing-room behind closed shutters, was utterly crushed and gave no sight of reaction to Marie's presence; she scarcely even recognized her.

'I did not want him to make the journey alone, Madame, after the shock he had this morning.'

Mother stared at me: 'Was it a shock for you?'

'More terrible than you can imagine: it was I who frightened the child, it was the sight of me that made her panic.'

Mother said listlessly: 'What are you talking about?' But she very soon paid closer attention. When I had done, she said: 'Now that the culprit has been caught and has confessed, there's no point in your talking; it must all remain between ourselves.'

'No,' Marie protested, 'it's important for the wretched man whose life is at stake. Alain's evidence will prove that the child was in fact terrified, that she ran into the wood and that it all happened just as the man described it, though they didn't believe him: the little girl was panting, out of breath . . .'

'Yes,' I said, 'that breathlessness must have done for her.'

I wanted to go to the police immediately, but they were all up at
the mill, so Mother told me; the murderer was showing them where
he had thrown the body. I refused to wait. And Mother said to
Marie: 'You won't leave him?'

The police took less interest in me than I had expected. They had
got the murderer, and they were going to retrieve the body. The
inspector who questioned me seemed to attach no importance to
what I had to tell him about the terror that the child must have felt
at the sight of me. The matter was closed, as far as they were concerned. When I came home I slept for two hours, heavily. I learned
later that while I was asleep Mother and Marie had talked about me,
or rather that Marie had sought to arouse Mother's concern about
me. She must have felt she had succeeded, since she left for the station
at six o'clock without seeing me again: 'but,' Mother declared, 'with
her mind at ease about you.'

Mother's newly-awakened anxiety distracted her a little from the
haunting vision of that small corpse. I discovered during the night
she spent by my side, in Laurent's bed, that she had been bound to
the Séris girl by other links than the sordid calculations I had
ascribed to her, that she loved the motherless child and had been
loved by her.

'But what you did not know, what you could not know since I
was not allowed to speak of her to you, was the extent of her love
for you.'

'Her love for me?'

'Yes, it seemed unbelievable in a twelve-year-old girl. I'd never
have imagined such a thing could exist, or else I'd have been shocked
by it, if I had not seen for myself how she worshipped you, with a
tender devotion that was none the less a woman's love, yet utterly

pure and innocent, as I well know, since she talked about you incessantly to me. If there's one thought that can help me not to revolt against the horror of what that innocent child endured, it is that now she can see that you no longer hate her, that you mourn for her, that you won't forget her, that you no longer think of her as the Louse . . .'

'But she didn't know that I called her the Louse?'

'She knew. She hadn't learnt it from me, needless to say. Numa Séris had heard it from the Dubercs, from your precious Simon I suppose, and one night when he was drunk he told the child. She cried, she cried bitterly . . .'

And now it was the two of us who were crying in the darkness, Mother and I, with our hearts full of that intolerable reality of what the child had endured in her poor little body, so soiled and defiled.

'Alain, you who have read so many books, who know all that people have written about the evil that God allows, why should a child, a little girl, have been handed over, body and soul, to a blind beast before her death? What's the sense of such an ordeal, which children endure every day? And even so we only know what we learn from the press. But every day, everywhere, throughout the world . . .'

She fell silent, awaiting my answer. I went on weeping over that small dishonoured corpse which all the water in the Hure could not cleanse. At last I said:

'Perhaps evil is a person . . .'

'Then he must exist, he must have been created, and given that power.'

'Maman, there is no other answer than that naked body, for it was naked, spurned and spat upon and nailed to a gibbet, despised by intellectuals, which was our Saviour's body. The little girl knows the answer, she holds it close to her heart, now and for evermore. And we shall know, presently, that of which we have an inkling each time we communicate with that despised, crucified and glorious body.'

'Yes, I believe it, I believe it . . .'

I heard her sob, for the first time in my life; she was weeping for love.

'I loved that little girl as I've never loved anyone else, not even yourself. I had told her: "you've got to be educated, I've never been able to talk to Alain about anything. None of the women in our set are his equal." So, having left primary school after taking her *certificat d'études*, she had begun to study with our schoolteacher, who's a most intelligent man, and who is working for his *licence de lettres*. She was learning Latin, too, with M. le curé, who had opened her mind to the questions that interest you. He knows about such things now; poor M. le Doyen, you've no idea how much you have influenced him. I'm preventing you from sleeping. My darling, you must get some sleep.'

'What matters most to me isn't sleeping, it's having you there.'

We remained for a while without speaking. The autumnal night wind gave a voice to the Maltaverne pine trees and they wept with us over the fate of that child, flung a live prey to a wild beast, not to be devoured like the maiden Blandine but to be as foully defiled as one of God's creatures can be on this earth, and the last sight she had seen had been that dreadful face. Mother spoke again:

'If I'm to believe that young woman' (meaning Marie), 'you had got it into your head that I had ordered the poor child to spy on you in my absence. How could you have believed me capable of . . . It's true that I told her too many things. We lived so close to one another during my visits to Maltaverne, when you weren't there! She knew how anxious I had been ever since that young woman came into your life. In fact we talked about nothing but you. But if the child kept watch on you during your stay, it was not because I'd asked her to, it was of her own free will, on her own account. I

could never have believed it possible that a girl of that age should
be as jealous as she was. What she suffered because of you, that
evening and that night, she told me, for she used to tell me everything. We told each other everything. I wasn't jealous myself, you
know. I would have given my life for you to love her. She believed
you would end by loving her and she made me believe it. The
horrible thing is that it was true, that you loved her one hour before
she was raped and strangled . . .'

'Yes, and I shall love her now to the end of my days, I shall
cherish her within me, I shall hold her close to my heart, poor little
Louse, my only love.'

Suddenly I heard Mother laugh. Yes, she was laughing. She said:
'Do you know how she revenged herself for being called the Louse?
She always called that young woman the "clutcher" because she'd
often heard me worry that you were in her clutches.'

This time the silence between us remained unbroken, and then I
heard my mother's sleeping breath, almost a groan, as if it had been
drawn through all the tears she still had to shed. I lay there wakeful,
retracing in my mind the path we had already travelled, which was
like the road to Calvary: the first station being my brother's death,
the second the rape of that child. Weak and defenceless as I was, how
should I find strength to take another step forward? Ah, I longed to
be lying on the bare ground, in a corner of Maltaverne that I know
and that I used to call Beauty when I was a child, I don't know why.
To lie there and wait till I fell asleep, never to wake again.

At last I slept too. When I awoke Mother was no longer in the
room. She must have gone out to Mass. I made no attempt to pray,
not from any spirit of revolt but because a disaster like this creates
a sense of absence – not indeed of non-existence, but it seems impossible that anyone should be there, and yet He is there; that's the
mystery of faith, indestructible in those on whom that grace has

been bestowed, able to withstand even the murder of a little girl, and a murder like this one, the very thought of which made me want to howl monotonously like a tortured animal.

Each of us, on waking, withdrew once more into imprisoning anguish. To avoid journalists (my statement had appeared in the press) I went into hiding in our shooting-box at La Chicane, which is remote and inaccessible. In fact, now that the murderer was behind bars and had confessed, the story had already been replaced by others. The whole problem was to find strength to carry on, to decide what direction to take. Marie wrote me that I ought to leave for Paris as soon as I felt strong enough:

'. . . that uprooting which your favourite Barrès denounces as an evil is the only remedy, after the shock you have endured, brings you the only hope of a cure. Of course everything that has happened will dwell within you wherever you are, yet you may perhaps have the gift, which you so much admire in others, of rediscovering it alive, of exhuming it. That is what Simon Duberc thinks about you, saying with monotonous but finally impressive conviction: "He'll be great some day, you'll see!" I love him for that, in spite of that streak of coarseness, the perverted peasant side of him, in spite of the monster you made of him at Maltaverne – he believes in you. He does not love you as much a you imagine, he may even detest you at certain moments, but he believes in you. It's the faith that others have in us that shows us the way we must go. Simon and I, after Donzac, are showing you your way, apart from which there is no right road for you.

'The only obstacle is your mother's attitude, and I'm the last person who would urge you to slight her. If I feel any remorse when I think of our time together it is on her account – I had formed a shockingly simplified mental image of her, based on what you and Simon had said of her. You remember that I used to say, during her repeated visits to Maltaverne, that she was "betraying you with your estates". Well, today we know that she was betraying you with Jeannette Séris – for it was a case of real love, although neither sex nor kinship was involved.'

Yes, I could see it at last: an ageing woman had poured out on to a small girl all the affection which nobody, all her life long, had needed, except a husband who probably repelled her physically, and myself, whom she could never understand, who seemed of a different race although born of her body; by my mere presence I deepened the abyss of loneliness in which poor 'Madame' would have foundered but for the property which kept her head above water, and the pious rites that marked out her days . . . But there had been that child whom I had hated, and who had loved me, and whom Mother loved.

Yes, this was not an obstacle to be skirted. Mother approved of my wish to go to Paris, but she wanted me to wait another year. I had admitted that the preliminary work for my thesis could be done at Bordeaux. But, far more than my thesis, my very life was at stake, or so I had convinced myself. I had to gamble on this last chance, to uproot myself from a land where I had been wounded to the heart, and try the experiment of replanting myself in unfamiliar soil – driven by an idea which was derived not only from Donzac, from Simon, from Marie, but perhaps, too, from the businessmen who were my forebears: the idea of turning to good account the dreadful experience I had gained, of letting none of it go to waste. 'Waste nothing,' we used to be told as children, but that was a matter of scraps of bread or candle-ends. Now, for me, the thing that must not be wasted was the suffering I had endured and con- ferred, it was the child's body flung by her murderer into that alder-fringed stream which would go on flowing within me until the last hour of my life, it was the crushing personality of my mother, now herself crushed. That was the capital on which I now had to live. Everything that might happen to me henceforward, however endless my journey, would remain outside the fateful circle that had been traced around this part of my life.

Mother said to me: 'Whatever they say, one doesn't die of grief. People don't die of their grief. Even if they are never comforted, they don't die. But I shall die, I have begun dying. Wait a little, don't leave me.' I could not tell her that for me, at twenty-two, things were not so simple and that I had to try and survive. I used to take with me to La Chicane, every day, one volume from my father's set of Balzac – the Charpentier edition of 1839, containing certain titles which have not been reproduced in the complete works. Balzac is not my favourite writer: he is too coarse, I mean as regards style. But he is the author who acts most directly upon me as a stimulus to want to go on living. I detest the race of ruthless, ambitious young men that he depicts, and yet they make me want to try my luck, like them, but in my own way, which I yet have to discover.

For the time being I am still confined within the circle; this is not something past, to be rediscovered and transposed, it's not an experience that has been lived through, it is what I am living through here and now, and Maman is there, still alive, and I cannot let her die alone, haunted by the defiled, staring-eyed image of the little girl she loved. She told me: 'Every moment of my days and nights I see her dead, her eyes dilated with terror.'

She paid daily visits to old Séris, who was drinking less than she had feared because he wanted to settle his business affairs 'before getting down to serious drinking'.

'Would you believe it,' Mother said, 'at that funeral service where everyone was in tears, your grief was the only thing that seemed to touch old Séris. He might have borne you a grudge, even if he does not know how much the child suffered on your account. Well, it wasn't so; and do you know what he suggested? A fictitious sale of his whole estate, so that you would in fact be his heir, the little girl's heir . . .'

'Not for the world,' I protested.

'Of course,' Maman said. 'There can be no question of that. I was so sure of your refusal that I refused in both our names, convinced that you'd agree. Then he proposed a real sale, with himself retaining the life interest. It's for you to decide.'

'But Maman, I'll do whatever you want.'

'What I want? I want nothing at all. The very thought of benefiting by the child's death appals me. The Séris estate will be divided between his various nephews, and there'll be nothing left of it. That's what I should like: for nothing to be left of what was hers. I wish it could all be burnt. Moreover that's what Numa Séris believes will happen, it'll all be destroyed by fire in the end.'

'Why should it all burn more readily than at any time in the past, Maman? From time immemorial the alarm-bell has sounded and the fire has been got under control . . .'

'Just because, according to Séris, if the alarm-bell rings in the years to come there'll be nobody to answer it; the farms will all be deserted. People will be increasingly unwilling to live like wild animals in those out-of-the-way places, on black bread and corn mush. Séris says that American scientists have found out how to extract turpentine without the use of our resin, and that there will be less and less demand for our pine trees for mine-props and railway sleepers. So it will all be burnt up,' Mother repeated with a sort of desperate satisfaction, 'because there'll be nobody left . . . And why should the trees be allowed to survive? They will die too, they'll be burnt alive. It'll be better than . . .

'You believed that I loved the land for its own sake. What I dreamed of was yourself and that child owning it all, and myself keeping watch over the pair of you, over your interests, and seeing her being happy with you. When the Doyen scolded me, repeating: "you won't take your farms with you!" I would tell him: "but I shall rejoice on my deathbed at knowing that the children will own them, and that I'm leaving them the land in the best state possible." I used to tell him that property endures, that it is injured by partition, but is increased through marriage and inheritance, and can defy death. I know now that this is not true. But what is true, Alain, what is true?'

Nothing remained for me but to put myself in God's hands and await a sign from Him – that sign which might perhaps be a summons, heard by me alone, to anticipate my appointed hour. It meant disregarding what was going on inside my mother, unknown to myself and to her: yes, literally, what was 'going' within her, what was changing, and was about to take shape in that unexpected decision of hers which has set me free.

On All Saints' Day we went to lay flowers on Jeannette's grave. I was struck by the fact that Mother did not recite the *De Profundis*, as she used to do when she made us kneel, Laurent and myself, on our poor father's grave. 'Out of the depths have I cried to Thee, Lord, Lord . . .' Was it the pathos of this entreaty that her voice unconsciously conveyed? or was it my own anguish expressed by that voice? Now, on this latest All Saints' Day, no cry rose from the abyss on whose edge my mother stood, like an ancient oak tree, still green although struck by lightning. She did not kneel down, her lips did not move. On the way home she said to me:

'I have just made up my mind. I shan't go back to Bordeaux. I shall wait here. So you can go to Paris, as that young woman said the day she brought you home: "he's got to go to Paris", she kept telling me.'

'But wait for what, Maman?'

She said once more: 'I shall wait . . .' I reminded her that she would not have M. le Doyen, who was going to end his days in Bordeaux, not in charge of some parish as he had always hoped and expected, but as chaplain to a convent.

'I know that, and I've no great hopes of his successor.'

We had not yet made his acquaintance; he had refused to call on us before he had visited all the poorest farms in the parish. He had unkindly made clear to the poor Doyen his firm resolve not to become 'the gentry's priest'.

'Hunger brings the wolf out of the woods,' Mother said, 'and it won't be long before he comes a-begging. As for the farmers, they'll send for him as they usually do, to bless their pigstyes. Anyhow, M. le Doyen thinks his successor is quite right, that we've been making a mistake, that we've made mistakes about everything.'

She was stepping out firmly along the road, returning the greetings of those she met with nods and smiles proportionate to their importance, and yet what she chiefly suggested to me at this point in her life was that fly which a schoolfellow of mine, pretending to degrade Dreyfus, had gradually dismembered. Thus Mother was being stripped, day by day, of all her certainties. Nothing was true of all that she had believed, but the falsest thing of all was what she had mistaken for revealed truth. Even if she were not clearly conscious of this, she was enduring it now as an undeniable fact, with the bleak insensibility of a creature afflicted through the child she has loved above all else in the world; all the rest may be taken from her, she can feel nothing more.

'When everything fails us, when we feel utterly forlorn, at that moment that always comes for each one of us, when in our turn we sigh: "My God, why hast Thou forsaken me?" the hour of the final defeat which the Cross foreshadows, of which the Cross is the symbol, shocking and intolerable to anyone in the morning or noonday of life, until the time when it becomes that which corresponds exactly to one's own body . . .'

Mother broke in: 'And to one's heart.'

I was astonished to hear these words from her. How did she know that it is always one's heart that is crucified? Perhaps she had had an emotional life of which we knew nothing. Her affection for Jeannette must have been heralded by other affections. I tried to remember. All that I could recall was that after my father's death, in the old town house where scarcely anybody came, we were visited once or twice a year by a schoolfriend of Mother's, Sarah M . . ., an Irish or English woman, accompanied by a little girl – her ward, Mother told us. They would come from afar, like sea birds driven inland by the equinoctial gales. The birth of this little girl, Andrée, was linked to one of those secrets about which Mother would say: 'it doesn't concern you.' Nothing concerned us, but everything became part of my life and none of it will be wasted.

The last rearguard action Mother fought was to ask me to stay in a Catholic student's hostel in Paris; but I assured her that at twenty-two I was too old for that, that the fact of knowing nobody in Paris did not alarm me, indeed it put me on my mettle; I wanted to start from scratch, to try and storm the great city like so many country boys before me, without one letter of introduction in my pockets.

'But what sort of life will you lead?'

'I presume, the life of an industrious student, careful to let no chances slip. And I look forward, above all, to certain chance encounters.'

Mother asked: 'For good or for evil?'

'Things are never so simple. I believe that all our encounters, even the worst, are willed.'

'What do you know about it, my poor lad?'

What, indeed, did I know about it? It was I who deliberately read a meaning into my story, arranged it to suit my own ideas, ascribed human purposes to the infinite Being; and my inventions satisfied myself alone.

Mother had stopped listening to me. She was asking me what sum she should send me each month, and could not accept my reply that she need not concern herself about it, that I needed no intermediary to dispose of my own property. Until the end, she would control my expenses, and spend every Sunday afternoon poring over her account books.

XIII

November was a radiant month. Mother was to go with me to Bordeaux, help me to pack my trunk and return alone to Maltaverne; she had made up her mind; but I kept telling her that I did not want to decide anything beforehand, that I would stay beside her if I thought it necessary, although it was obvious that I could do nothing more to help her. She did not even pretend to protest.

A couple of days before the date of our departure she asked me to go with her to M. Lapeyre's mill-pond. I confessed that I, too, had wanted to make this pilgrimage, but that my courage had failed me.

'Together,' she said, 'we can do it.'

She was wearing her town hat and her black gloves and had opened her parasol. She was not in mourning, she had no right to wear mourning for Jeannette, to whom she was not related, but her dress now bore no trace of holiday informality, as if the dead child, who was always with her, required her to maintain a constant ceremoniousness.

Mother, who was very little given to walking in ordinary life, proceeded with a certain majesty along the sandy path, which was carpeted with pine needles. When we drew near to the mill she took my arm, a thing she normally never did.

'It was from here I saw her,' I said. 'At first I took her for a boy.'

She stopped. She looked at the still, unruffled water of the mill-dam. She asked me to take her into the bracken to the place where I had been sitting.

'I think it was here. Yes, this is the place '

She stood there, her face turned towards the sleeping water, and I saw her, who had never shed a tear in our presence, once again touch her eyes with the back of her gloved hand. She said: 'Lend me your handkerchief.'

'We must go back, Maman, let's go back the quickest way.'

She gave no answer, but left the wood and moved towards the dam. No, it was impossible that she should have experienced such a temptation. I took her arm, but she shook it free. For a few endless minutes I stared at the distorted reflection in the water of my mother in her town hat and gloves, under her open parasol. 'Let's go home,' she said at last.

We followed the sandy track along which Jeannette Séris had taken her last steps on earth. I had to explain to Mother from how far off I could see her walking sedately, or running and playing – poor little Red Riding Hood.

'Ah,' she murmured, 'here's the turning towards which she ran when she caught sight of you . . .'

'Yes, and that's the way she went into the wood.'

As if she were trying to trail a wild creature, Mother questioned me, staring at the ground: 'Are you sure this was where she went into the wood?' She did not venture in. She stood motionless among the bracken, her face turned towards the pine trees which had witnessed . . I tried to take her hand, but she withdrew it, and without turning her head, said in a low voice:

'It was because she was afraid of you. If you had merely been indifferent to her, as a lad of your age might naturally have been towards a little girl, she would not have thought of running away, nothing would have happened, she would still be alive. To have felt such terror she must have been aware of your hatred.'

'No, Maman, no! She knew, and she could only have learnt of it through you, that I disliked the idea of a marriage prearranged for reasons of interest . . .'

'It was not for reasons of interest. It was you who attributed such motives to me.'

'You never told me anything that could make me believe you had others . . .'

'Because you hated her so much that I dared not even utter her name in front of you. As soon as I opened my mouth you'd have made me shut up, you'd have marched out slamming the door. She knew that you called her by that foul nickname. That was what killed her. Yes, she was mortally wounded before she ever went into that wood. You had cut her to the heart long ago.'

'Mother, you're too unjust.'

I tried to seize her arm but she pushed me away almost violently and walked on alone, while I followed close on her heels, repeating: 'you're unjust, too unjust!' Then she half turned her head and said defiantly: 'Yes, it was you, it was you!'

'Can't you see, my poor mother, that if I'm to be held responsible for this tragedy so, above all, must you be, since you did your best to make me loathe your plans. In the past you had always decided everything for me, but after all I still had the whole of my life to live, I'm twenty-two, and you claimed the right to dispose of it according to your own notions, and in spite of what you say it was always a matter of the Séris estate. Never, at any time, could I have suspected your affection for the child . . .'

'Because I was afraid of irritating you still more if you'd known that I loved her . . .'

'Better than myself?'

She made no reply. When we reached Maltaverne she climbed up the perron slowly, pausing on every step. In the hall she repulsed me again:

'You must leave me alone. I need nobody any more. Understand me: nobody.'

.   .   .   .   .

I heard her bedroom door close, and I went near the fire. The wind had got up and the branches that it shook seemed to be waving to me through the windows. A vast, confused lamentation blended with that silent cry within me, that heartfelt, despairing reproach to God.

I did not light the lamp. What decision could I take? Mother not only did not need me now, my presence had actually become hateful to her. None the less I had to look after her, to remain within reach in case she should call for help. Her resentment would inevitably diminish, and she would have recourse to me because she had nobody else but me. Yes, but if she should refuse to leave the place, what was to become of me? Must we stay closeted together at Maltaverne for a whole winter, or should I live alone in the Rue de Cheverus, waited on by Louis Larpe?

These thoughts followed one another with no sort of logic during the indefinite period while I sat by the fire, with no lamp lit, and the twilight darkened, and I could make out nothing but the two pale patches that were my two hands lying on my thin knees. And then I heard my mother's slow, heavy step on the stair. It was not time for our evening meal yet; she must be coming back to me. She came into the room. I did not rise from my armchair. She laid one hand on my hair and drew it back from my forehead, as she used to when I was a child, for our goodnight kiss; but this evening there was no kiss. She spoke to me, however, with a deliberate gentleness which was unlike her.

'We must forget what we have said to one another, my poor child. We have been unfair to each other. I used to be hurt when you declared that there was no communication between us, that we had never really talked to each other as people do in plays and novels. Well, we've made up for that now, on the way back from the mill.'

'Yes, it all poured out of us involuntarily.'

'What poured out of us, of me at any rate, must be forgotten. I was looking for someone to complain of, someone on whom I could lay the blame. And so were you . . . We were each accusing the other. . . .'

'Yes,' I said gloomily, 'like two accomplices at the Assize Court.'

She said: 'Don't talk like that!' I could not see her, but I could hear her weeping. I got up, put my arms round her and asked her to forgive me.

'None of it was our fault, Maman; whatever depended on us could not have given rise to anything worse than a misunderstanding which would eventually have been cleared up, which would quickly have been cleared up, for I was eager to discover who was the girl I had seen bathing, and I should have found it out that evening but for Simon's telegram.'

'It would have made no difference. Everything had already happened.'

'Yes, Maman, and neither you nor I played the slightest part in this incredible coincidence. But crimes of this sort are always due to some chance meeting. You can always say: "if the child had taken a different path . . ."'

She murmured: 'It's done now. It has happened, it has been done . . .' We sat in silence. I could only make out a blurred mass in the chair facing me.

'Listen, Alain, let's speak frankly, with no beating about the bush. There's no question but that you must go. It'll be better for both of us. You can write to me often; we shall irritate one another less by letter. You can tell me about your life, at least that part of your life that you can tell me about. I'll look after your business affairs; if I were to fall ill, a telegram would be enough, the car would be waiting for you at Bordeaux and you could be here the same evening.'

'Yes, from a distance you'd be able to put up with me, you'd get used to me again . . .'

This time, too, she made no protest. Had she heard, had she understood? She asked:

'Have you really decided to leave the day after tomorrow? In any case you'll have to spend a day in Bordeaux.'

'No, Maman. I've got all the books here that I need to take. The car can take me directly to the Paris train. It leaves at four minutes past eleven.'

'But your clothes are almost all in the Rue de Cheverus . . .'

'I have here all that is necessary for the life I want to lead at first, as a student who will be invited nowhere because he knows nobody.'

'You'll make some friends eventually.'

'Maybe. But if I'm to go into society I must first notice how people dress in Paris. You remember the mortification of poor Lucien de Rubempré when he landed in Paris dressed in the fashion of Angoulême.'

She asked under her breath, as though not expecting an answer: 'Who is Lucien de Rubempré?'

'Come, Maman! You've read *Les Illusions Perdues*! I made you read it!'

'Oh, you know, I'm not like you; I don't retain anything that I've read, it runs straight through my head . . .'

She began to poke the fire, with her elbows on her knees, as I had so often seen her do, and she suddenly said to me:

'You ought to telegraph to that young woman to meet you at the station and see you on to the train.'

'No, Maman, I no longer need anyone to see me on to the train. In any case I loathe stations almost as much as graveyards. My new life will begin the day after tomorrow at four minutes past eleven. That is when I shall be reborn.'

Prudent's wife came to tell us that dinner was served.

'To think,' Mother said, as she got up, 'that I'm hungry, that I shall be glad to eat.'

We sat opposite one another under the hanging lamp, which was smoking and smelt of oil. I felt a sudden sense of joy at the thought that I was going off so soon to another world, another life.

No, it was not joy, but that impatience that one feels in an endless, stifling tunnel: the need to get out of it at all costs, as fast as possible escaping for ever without a backward look, and with all one's treasure within oneself.

Mother got up heavily, and we went back to our armchairs. She laid a log on the fire and turned up her skirts, as I had so often seen her do, to warm her legs at the fire. Suddenly she said without looking at me:

'The more I think of it, the more I feel it's only right that you should let that young woman know you are leaving, and tell her the time of your train.'

'It's odd, you must admit, my poor dear mother, that it should be you who . . .'

I broke off in time, for fear of adding, however slightly, to her suffering.

'Yes,' she said, 'I thought ill of her. I thought of her as the person who threatened my little girl's happiness. I never imagined, poor fool that I was, that the thing that was to destroy that happiness would first destroy my poor little girl herself, and how it was going to happen. Everything looks so different to me today, people and things . . . Or rather I see them as they really are, neither worse nor better. Oh, it's no longer going to be hard for me to obey the precept "judge not". No, I shan't judge anyone any more. And besides I know that young woman better than you think. I never told you all we said to one another, she and I, during those two hours while you were asleep, utterly knocked out after making your statement to the police. She was not play-acting, I can tell you. She had only one thought in her head: that I must not lose sight of you, because she believed you to be suffering from a complaint she had seen at close quarters in the person of that priest who played so important a part in her life. I understand what she must have been to you and what she could still be; and after all it may as well be her as someone else! She could do what I did myself, she would protect you, watch over you without asking anything in return. You told me once that she had suffered more than any other girl of her age; well, I know now what that means: she had crossed the line beyond which there's nothing left; I'm an old woman, but I still lived on my hopes, I hated whatever threatened them. But now . . . why not her, after all? I can still carry on, after a fashion, for a little while; but I shan't go far. You'll be left alone. So why not her?'

'No, Mother, don't begin again, don't let's begin again. I've got to uproot myself from my death-in-life here, and I'm going to uproot myself from it. If it kills me, the sooner the better. But it won't! I shall live! I shall live!'

'You are ungrateful, as you have always been. The young woman knows that now, as I've always known it.'

'She gave me what only she could give me, and I shall never forget it, as long as I live. But understand, Maman, I myself have crossed the line beyond which one no longer seeks to be happy, but to gain control over one's life. I have crossed that line at twenty-two, and you at over sixty.'

This was what I said to Mother, two days before I left for Paris. But it has become written language. Since I began keeping this diary I have instinctively transposed my experiences, without ulterior motive, because I always had a gift for narrative at school and because I was following in the tracks of my industrious school-boy self. Now the time has come for me to look squarely and unashamedly at that temptation to which I cannot yield until Mother is gone: that the outcome of all this agony will be a three-franc paperback. The new man born within me must show his strength and courage by daring to exploit for his own advancement those experiences which will have become the substance of a three-franc paperback.

I remember nothing of our further talk during that long vigil, before we went up silently to our bedrooms (carrying the same old oil lamps, since the electric light could not be switched off from the first floor): I had probably listened inattentively to it; what I was then facing was the truth that I had never yet clearly defined to myself: that for me, giving up my mother and giving up Marie were part of the same need; not the result of a selfish or cruel nature nor of any lack of feeling for others. The impulse now taking shape within me, which I would follow with cold determination, was due to a wish to survive, and this twofold renunciation was its essential condition.

I lay for a long while shivering between my icy sheets, in that country bedroom during that night in late autumn, and I thought things over methodically. The oil lamp was still burning, but its narrowly circumscribed glow left the room submerged in a shadow that harboured the ghosts of the dead and the living, and I wondered whether the absolute anonymity of an hotel bedroom in Paris would suffice to lay them. Not that I was afraid of them, but I could only live that new, unknown life by keeping them dormant within me, so that they should not divert me from the struggle I was resolved to wage.

I should not remain alone, I knew that. I should be loved, I was sure of it. But I had already determined that nobody should assume responsibility for me. My self-portrait is black enough; I don't need to darken it still further. I had no thought that night of exploiting others, of making use of them for my own success or pleasure. I do not know what the Lord meant by the sin against the Holy Ghost, which was for Him the irremissible sin, but I know, I have always known, what the sin against the body is. The strangling and rape of little Jeannette is only the foul and inordinately magnified image of the spiritual crime committed with impunity by so many creatures who do not feel themselves responsible and who in fact perhaps are not. But I, my God, whatever I may do, am responsible to You. I shall strive to become pure again because I cannot do without You – ah, that I know! You know: born in different surroundings, I might perhaps have been able to do without everything else but not without You.

Such was the theme of my prayers that night, my penultimate night at Maltaverne: I drifted between past time and time to come, between what I had suffered and what I was going to suffer, which was bound up with encounters, failures, misunderstandings, sicknesses and events which could not be foreseen. I thought of nothing but my own personal story, as though the history of my country did not concern me.

I have begun writing again, in a room that is as silent as my room at Maltaverne. Its window opens on to the narrow garden of the Hôtel de l'Espérance, in the Rue de Vaugirard, opposite the Carmelites' seminary. The rumble of the Paris street is more muffled than the soughing of the pine trees in the park under the equinoctial gales; I am calm, I am not in distress. Yesterday morning, which was Sunday, I sold Sangnier's paper La Démocratie outside the church door at Saint-Sulpice. I had been to register in the Boulevard Raspail the very day after my arrival. This was the first task they gave me to do, in spite of my title of licencié ès-lettres, of which I believe I boasted for the first time. They were probably right to make me undergo this ordeal, which proved decisive: they will see me no

more. Five or six years ago, I should have consented to it; it's too
late today. So, for the time being, I do nothing but haunt libraries,
put down my name for courses, attend lectures, a student like all the
rest of them, with no outward sign of what I bear within me, which
no doubt is not a heavier burden than many of them have to carry –
but this matter is my responsibility and no one else's. I alone am
capable of seeing that none of it is wasted, of letting nothing run to
waste of my youth which was different from anyone else's, richer
and yet bleaker than any other and, above all, lonelier; and then,
however few the characters in my story, what other young man has
had a mother like mine, and what other carries in his heart the image
of a defiled and strangled child?

The final pages of this notebook must give a clear answer to a
question which seems simple and yet which, ever since I came to
Paris, I have been eluding. André Donzac lives opposite my hotel in
the Carmelite seminary, and he thinks I am still in Bordeaux. Why
have I not made contact with him? At first I trusted to a chance
meeting which I thought inevitable, as if the Rue de Vaugirard had
been the Rue de Cheverus! In fact, I dread such a meeting. Why? I
know that I shall have to bring it about; I need to be introduced to
the Sorbonne, and not by a hasty and indifferent guide but by a
friend like Donzac, who knows what sort of creature I am, who will
look after me as long as need be – introduced, too, to libraries and
also to museums. I am living within a stone's throw of the Luxem-
bourg, of that Caillebotte collection which I know André visits
almost daily, and which he made me swear not to visit without him;
he wants to be there when I see Manet's *Balcon* for the first time. I
can wait. I'm not impatient; the streets, in Paris, have more to offer
than any museum.

In fact I have a more urgent reason for seeking out Donzac: I am
anxious to retrieve my notebooks, which are in his keeping. This is
all-important to me! Supposing that old seminary building should

burn down, supposing Donzac should die suddenly . . . Is it crazy to
stake one's whole life on a boyhood diary? And yet that is what I am
doing. Thank God there's no one else on earth who knows that and
can laugh at it.

And then I have to find something to fill out the four pages of my
weekly letter to my mother. States of mind are no use for her, one's
got to have what she calls 'something to tell'. Hitherto I have only
talked about the hotel, how I am fed and looked after. Her two
brief answers have dealt with her health and a sale of timber.

But let's look a little deeper. Donzac belongs, for the time being
at any rate, to that sandy soil of the *lardes* from which I have
uprooted myself in order not to die. As soon as we meet, I am afraid
lest his mere presence should break the spell of Paris. How can I
define its magic, its intoxicating charm? I immerse myself in the
flood of humanity, I let it bear me along, I drift on the surface of
pavements, or dive into underground bars such as the Taverne du
Panthéon, at the corner of the Rue Soufflot and the Boulevard
Saint-Michel. In Bordeaux I was young Gajac, who was afraid of
other people; but in Paris I am nobody, I am as unknown as any
human being can be: nameless, even if I cannot be faceless – and it's
true that *chasseurs de visage* abound here, but I am not afraid of them,
since in a pursuit of that sort the quarry must be an accomplice and
that, I know, I shall never be.

So I walk by night, as far as my legs can carry me. Oh, I know
now why I trained for so many years, walking through the woods at
Maltaverne to find the old pine tree or visit the old man of Lassus!

The first evenings, I did not cross the Seine. I leaned on the parapets of the bridges – those parapets which I love for the sake of
Baudelaire and Maurice de Guérin who used to lean there, and of
so many characters in fiction! I would recite *le Bateau Ivre* (having
only this year discovered Rimbaud) and Victor Hugo, who is

present in every stone of the place. And then one evening I crossed over the river, and now I cross over it almost every evening. Near the entrance-gates of the Louvre, close to the palace wall, there are stone benches where nobody sits by night. I stop for breath there, gazing at that illustrious setting – but in 1907 Stéphen Pichon, Briand, Barthou (although, it's true, there were Clemenceau and Picquart too) were Lilliputian figures performing in that Shakespearian décor. I go up the Rue de Rivoli as far as the Concorde. Here again the stage stands empty, as though between the acts; in 1907, nothing was happening. What was about to happen I, who was twenty-two, would witness! I have always been crazy about history without knowing it; Paris has made me aware of my passion. I stare at Gabriel's two palaces and at the seated cities, the figure of Strasburg with its crowns and its faded banners, sensing what lies in embryo in that Lilliput of 1907, and what I am going to see . . .

When I am at the end of my tether I stop at Weber's, the only big café that I dare enter apart from those in the Latin quarter. I have lost all that contemptible fear of spending money that possessed me in Bordeaux. I sometimes order a dozen oysters and a half-bottle of champagne. I don't know what I look like, or what people take me for. In fact I doubt whether I should have returned to the Weber but for the couple I saw there on my first evening and have seen there repeatedly ever since. The old woman arrives first. She has grey hair cut short like Joan of Arc's. Yes, an aged Joan of Arc is what she looks like. They bring her an *assiette anglaise*, a plate of cold meat, and a glass of beer. She smokes, with her eyes fixed on the doorway. The other arrives shortly before midnight, weary and hungry: what work had she been doing? She's another Joan of Arc, but a fair-haired one, and the right age for Joan of Arc. The second evening I saw her she looked at me, recognizing me. The old woman was watching her in the mirror.

To go home, I take one of the Urban Company's cabs, with

rubber tyres and lamps the same colour as those in the Vaugirard coach-house.

Sometimes the weather is too bad for me to venture beyond the Boulevard Saint-Michel. I avoid none of the cafés there except the d'Harcourt, where one is pestered by seedy, diseased prostitutes. On such evenings I become a prey to my basic obsession. The mystery of evil, which had been only a mental concept to me, swarms visibly about one. The brute who had assaulted the Séris child in the wood, near Lapeyre's mill-pond, seems here to be on the prowl everywhere; but each monster is watched by all the rest and roams unmasked, showing the wild eyes and hideous mouth that should be hidden.

I have not yet ventured as far afield as Montmartre. I know the Latin quarter and its fauna, I have grown used to it, but Montmartre frightens me. I often hear it talked about at the Panthéon bar which is always crowded, where anyone is liable to speak to you. I reply readily, being nobody.

And then I go to bed about two o'clock, sinking into a deeper sleep than I ever knew at Maltaverne where the cocks used to awaken me at dawn. In Paris, when I emerge from sleep, people have been at work for hours. It's too late to go to Mass, except on Sundays. I lunch at midday with the other students in the hotel: the only moment in the day when I speak to fellow-creatures who know my surname and my Christian name, and from which province I have come to Paris, and who hate Maurras or admire him, and in whom I take so little interest that I don't even see them.

And then I begin wandering again; but in the afternoon my ports of call are the churches, although I cover the same ground as at night – calling on You, my God, to account for the things that I have seen by night. I always start with Saint-Sulpice, making my way along the Rue Férou, that narrow street where my father lived as a student during the last year of the Third Empire. Inside the church again, my course is always unchanged: I turn right on entering and halt in front of Delacroix's fresco. I am both Jacob and the angel: here am I, struggling with myself; for though I seem to waver I am in fact upright and tense; I demand an answer, sitting behind the high altar, facing Pigalle's Virgin, which Donzac hates but which I love. I stay there as long as I can bear to, and then go out into the Rue Servandoni. I reach the quays, and then walk up beside the Seine as far as Notre-Dame. And here I plunge in, I immerse myself as I used to in Saint-André's at Bordeaux; but the human history which this place has witnessed hides God from me.

Sometimes I wake up before dawn. I hear a belated cab rattling over the wooden pavement. I feel then as if nothing more can happen to me in this world, that nothing more will happen to me, that there's nothing left to be eaten or drunk, that the one night on the balcony at Maltaverne with Marie, who loved me, is all that I shall ever have, and that I am like a beggar who has been given his pittance and has nothing more to expect from anyone – not even unhappiness, because I received my share of that, too, the day when that little girl ran along in front of me on the path from Lapeyre's mill, and then a dead twig snapped under my sandal and she turned round.

Something has happened, none the less, but it's so slight that I don't know how to put it down. Yesterday evening at Weber's the older Joan of Arc did not appear; she must have been ill; I did not expect the younger one to come. I kept watch on the door, however. She came in at her usual time, she sat down, she studied the menu as though she did not know she was going to order an *assiette anglaise*, and then she raised her eyes, she looked at me and she smiled.